ASHES IN THE WIND

ISLANDS OF ASH

LASHELL RAIN

This novel is a work of fiction.

All characters and events portrayed are products of the author's imagination and are used fictitiously.

Dear Reader,

This book contains mature content.

Material includes:

Battle Scenes, Blood, Loss, Mature Sexual Content, Grief, Violence & Death

Cover done by Miblart.

CONTENTS

To those who have ever felt defeated—
"we never fail, we either win or we learn."

Osparia
Heavensreach
Esora
The Dock Markets
Emelyns Village
Lintawa Bay
New Point Peak
Sirens Pass
Swamps of Illusion
Waters of Draynua
Ember
Westwell Harbor
Woodhaven
Imperial District
The Western Wyverns
Capital City
Espien Islands
Iron Isle Harbor
Magni Island

Ashes in the Wind

AN OSPARIA SERIES NOVELLA

By Lashell Rain

CHAPTER ONE

S weat beaded along my brow, gliding down my face, and dripped from my lips. I heaved, bending at the waist, tasting the salt of my labor as I tried to catch my breath.

"Again," he commanded.

My father and I had been practicing since before the sun crested over the horizon. We started with weapons. He taught me how to get an arrow to hit its mark then did the same with battle-axes and swords before moving on to bending.

My father always said an enemy would not care if you were tired. Every muscle in my body ached as I gathered myself back into my fighting stance, preparing to run the course again. Wooden posts jutted from the ground with bags stuffed with straw for heads—my targets. My enemies.

My father played as my moving mark. I took a deep breath, shook out my limbs, and pumped the blood flowing through my veins faster, using my bending as I concentrated. Raising my arms methodically, the water lifted from the two buckets by my feet. It swirled around my arms as I prepared my attack. With a flick of my wrist, water sliced through the air, drawing the heads off of the closest post-like men. Bolting forward, I rushed by the nearby trees, shooting thin streams of water through anything with a straw head or a wooden body.

"Water moving fast enough is as sharp as any blade," my father voiced through the trees from within the training course but remained hidden from my line of sight. "But the ability to wield both is your advantage, Eme. Use it." His voice rang from behind me and I turned, sending a crescent blade of water soaring through the air, taking out the remaining wooden dummies. My last target still mocked me, unseen.

I closed my eyes, letting my fae hearing heed my surroundings. I waited for the faintest brush of a step from my left as I pulled water from the soil under my feet that I had wielded before and blasted it into the direction of the sound. My father yelled as he smacked into a nearby tree. I clenched my fist, turning the water to ice, freezing him there as I manipulated it to my every command.

"Ah, come on, is that all you've got?" he taunted as he flexed a hand, using his own bending to melt the ice right off of him and sending the water hurling toward me again. I leaped, blocking his blow with a shield of my own water, drawing it up from the muddy ground. I tugged the axe from my hip in one swift motion as I dropped my shield and propelled it through the air. He tilted his head to the side as it grazed his face, causing him to stumble back into the tree. My father peered over his shoulder where my blade sat a mere inch from his cheek, sticking out of the wood. He looked at me with a wide smile.

"That's my girl," he declared, yanking the axe from the bark as he walked over to me.

"Orion, Emelyn!" My mother called us for lunch. He draped an arm over my shoulder, pulling me into his side as we sauntered back to our small cottage home.

"Good work today," he said, placing a kiss atop my head. My father stood over a foot taller than me, his frame strong from years of training.

Walking through the narrow paths of our village with a smirk on my face, I replied, "Thanks, Pada." *Father.* All the cottage homes sat alongside and behind each other in rugged rows, built with extended thin logs we'd chopped and molded ourselves with thatched roofs on top. Our home appeared, sitting on the outskirts where a break in the tree line ahead revealed the Heavensreach Mountains where the Sky Elves dwelled. Peering up, I could see them soaring through the open blue skies, preparing for the day's comings and goings. Flying seemed invigorating. I wondered what that kind of freedom would feel like, to soar the skies like the dragons and elves of Osparia.

A basin of water sat by our front door to clean up. My father washed his hands and splashed his face before I did the same. Smoke from the fire barrelled from our rooftop, floating into the canopy of trees as my mother prepared lunch for us inside. The smell of fish and herbs wafted through the air as my father opened the door for me to head in. My mother's long brown hair cascaded down her back. She had the top half pulled up and out of her face as she stood at the large, well-used wooden table to the side of the main room. She glanced over her shoulder at me.

"Foods almost ready. Did you get cleaned up?" she asked as I stepped over the threshold.

As my father walked up to her from behind and wrapped his arms around her waist, I replied, "yes, Ima." *Mother*.

"Mother moon," he murmured his curse into the crook of her neck. "Smells delicious, love," he said, placing a gentle kiss on her exposed shoulder. My mother's cooking was always delightful.

"Manners." She gave him a side-eye, a warning, but the look soon faded into a warm smile as my father leaned in for a quick peck on the lips. Seeing the affection my parents had for each other was something I wanted to have one day when I was older. Being mated was a blessing from the Mother herself. It wasn't a rarity. Most people found theirs, but it also wasn't a guarantee.

My mother turned out of my father's embrace and set the large prepared fish in the center of the table, caught fresh from the nets our people cast on our shores. My father grabbed the large knife and began chopping off its head. His usual.

"Gross," I exclaimed, scrunching my nose at him.

"The head is the best part. It's the richest for your body," he spoke, prodding the knife in my direction. "You'll appreciate it one day, Eme." He stabbed his portion and slapped it down on his plate. My mother poured water into the small cups already sitting on the table. I picked mine up to take it down in one swig. My father jabbed out his meal's eyes with his fingers and held them up to his own while sticking out his tongue, poking fun at me.

I couldn't hold back my snort, choking on my water. My nose burned as it shot through it and back out of me. My father chuckled while tossing one of his fish eyes into his mouth. I flicked my wrist in his direction, causing the water in his cup to douse him. I coughed and laughed as he wiped a hand down his damp face.

"Do you two ever stop playing?" my mother asked, her features serious. But as she glared at us, we all started laughing. She stood, readying to clean up the mess as my father devoured his fish.

"I got it, Ima." With a wave of my hand, the water lifted and shot out the small open window that sat above our counter full of stored food in containers and vegetables strung up on nobs along the weathered wall.

"Your water bending should be used for more important things, Eme." She sent a glaring eye at my father as she continued, "Not cleaning up puddles. It is a blessing from the Mother herself bestowed upon the people of Esora and should be treated as such." My mother reprimanded my laziness in her mastered tone.

She was the Kumai, *teacher,* for all the young fae in our homeland of Esora. The Kumai taught us of our history, our bending, and how to use it and respect it. I admired her wisdom.

My parents had told me the tales before bed growing up of how long ago, the god of the sun and the goddess of the moon waged war with one another until they finally made peace and blessed Osparia, restoring balance within our world, along with all the other stories of the creatures that lurked within the woods and waters of Osparia.

The water's call to me was indefinable, as if something rooted it in my bones and blood to use it. It was second nature, like eating or drinking. It came naturally, without a thought. But my mother could go about her day only using the work of her hands until she needed her bending for more vital things.

I nodded in understanding while I ate my portion as my father stood, his plate clean. His chair scuffed against the wooden slats as he pushed it back. He placed his hand over my mother's, leaning on the table.

"Cut her some slack, Ivy. She did well today." He gave me a wink as he stood up for me, and my mother rolled her eyes at him playfully. I covered my mouth, trying to hide my smile at my father's resilience.

"Why must I always be the villain of your fun?" my mother questioned.

"Because without your discipline, love, we'd lose our way." He gave my mother a wink and another quick kiss before turning away. "I need to go finish—" My father's statement got cut off by the door blowing open with a gust of wind. I jolted to my feet, one hand readying to wield any liquid near as my other gripped the axe at my side. My mother and father did the same, preparing for what lay beyond the door.

The burly man tucked his wings into his back and rushed in, his expression tense. I caught the fear in his azure eyes. I didn't think I'd ever see the day where a Sky Elf was afraid of something.

"Hallan . . ." My father's head tilted in question. "What is it, brother? What's wrong?" he asked in the midst of Hallan's stunned silence.

Hallan and my father's friendship went back to when I was only a babe. Now they were both leaders of their own people, each having a wife and child, Ace and me. We had grown up together but our lives stayed busy in our simple ways of living. There were constantly things to be done, which was why I hadn't seen him in a while. Worry filled me as I thought something had happened to him.

The fae of Esora and Sky Elves had always helped each other. We traded goods, food, skins, anything to help the other get by for as long as we had dwelled in Esora and they in Heavensreach. Whatever transpired wasn't good based on Hallan's tensed muscles and emotionless face.

"Ember is coming. They will not be taking prisoners. They're coming for blood." His tone was hollow, raw, as if he had been screaming before flying down here to deliver the news.

"How could you possibly know that?" my father questioned while Hallan pulled a letter from his leathers and handed it to him.

"A shadow crow delivered it moments ago."

"What?" My father's voice was small as he peered at the message, his eyes bouncing between every line. "The only person who can wield shadows is Ember's empress . . . ," he trailed off as he finished reading the letter.

"Orion, what does it say?" My mother's patience was wearing thin as she grabbed my father by the arm, wielding him to turn toward her.

"The Empress has sent us a warning. Ember is coming because the Emperor believes the chosen one is among the Sky Elves. He refuses to listen to reason. He wants nothing to stand in his way of conquering Osparia." My father spoke quickly to my mother, telling her what she needed to hear as he gathered his weapon from the table and sheathed it at his side and prowled to Hallan.

"Where are your women and children? We must get them out of here and somewhere safe."

"It's hopeless. The letter states they'll be here within a day, and who knows how long it took for the shadows to deliver it. Kali is warning our people now, but there isn't enough time, Orion. War is coming!" His voice boomed from him as he spoke to my father. Hallan, lost in his emotions, let them get the best of him in that moment. My mother's eyes brimmed with tears, but she held them back as her lip trembled.

"Ivy, leave, take Eme. Gather up as many wives and children as you can and you run." My mother's tears streamed down her cheeks at my father's words. My own pricked behind my eyes. He cupped her face, bringing her forehead to his, his clear blue eyes meeting her jaded green ones. "Go to Lintawa Bay, through the markets. Jump a ship and get out of here."

"I can't . . ." Her voice broke through the tears as she squeezed her eyes shut.

"You must, love, look at me." He was stern and brave, but my mother shook her head. She wasn't leaving her homeland, her people, her mate. "Damn the Mother!" my father cursed, running his hand through his brown hair that fell to his shoulders. "Hallan." My father turned to his comrade, his friend, his brother in arms. "Have you seen any warships?"

"My men are patrolling now and will report back soon," Hallan replied, meeting my father's eyes as his own stormed with emotion. "I came here to ask for your aid. I know the letter doesn't involve your people—"

"I'd never let you fight alone. But that's my choice. I will give my people the opportunity to make their own decisions."

"I understand." Hallan held his head high, his ears slightly longer and more pointed than my own. A common trait in the Sky Elves, along with their feathered wings. ·

My father's hand on my shoulder pulled my attention back to him. I sniffled and wiped my eyes before the tears had the chance to slip.

"Hallan, could you get Eme to the docks?"

"What?" I questioned, ripping away from his touch.

"You need to get out of here, Eme."

"I'm not leaving, Pada." My voice was firm. Hallan would have to drag me out of here with a fight and I'd still come running back. He would have to kill me before I left my people behind. My parents. Everything I had ever known.

My father exhaled deeply, looking to the ground, trying to think of what to say or do. After a long moment of pause, he spoke again.

"Fine." He looked to my mother and me. "Stay together. Gather our people, they have a decision to make. Meet back in the courtyard in an hour. Hallan and I have to find a way to hide their wives and children who won't be fighting." My father clutched us both, wrapping us in a rib-breaking hug, kissing us both on our heads before he rushed to the front door of our home with Hallan by his side.

He grabbed his leather harness from the nob hanging from the wall next to the door. He pushed his arms through and then buckled it around his chest, creating straps on his back for Hallan to grip during the flight back up the mountain.

My father glanced over his shoulder, peering at us one last time. He gave us a reassuring smile and nodded, even though his eyes were uncertain of what was to come. They both took off into a sprint toward the mountains before they leaped into flight.

My mother wrapped her arm around me and squeezed. I did the same, savoring her warmth, her scent, only for a moment before she nudged me toward the door. We ran to every cottage, every door, every child playing amongst the trees, telling the parents of what awaited them once they were in the courtyard.

Within the hour, every fae I knew in Esora stood in the courtyard, pouring out of it onto the paths surrounding our homes out into the woods. Scared faces of husbands, wives, and fae of all ages stretched as far as I could see. My father swooped down from the trees as Hallan released him and he landed gracefully. They stood side by side in the face of the murmuring crowd. My mother and I settled only a few feet in front of him as he prepared to speak.

"My people!" he roared into the crowd as everyone slowly quieted. His voice echoed against the canopy of trees.

"Ember is moving. Their problem is not with us. They are coming for our comrades of the skies. They believe Heavensreach has the chosen. But I believe anyone willing to take innocent lives is an enemy of mine. I have decided that I will not retreat in fear. That is my choice. You all have your own decisions to make. As your leader, brother, and friend, I come to all who are willing and capable and ask that you fight with me. With us." My father gestured to Hallan at his side. "If you choose to run, I won't fault you. The choice is yours." He peered around the crowd. Children wailed and mothers sobbed in the arms of their husbands, knowing this would separate them either by the war or by death to save their livelihoods. Their families. Their homelands.

A man called out from the front.

"Mai lao kahi." *Forever as one,* the man shouted in our mother tongue, holding his head high. Others accompanied him until they filled the woods with the declarations of our people. *As one.* My eyes stung from the amount of love I beheld within the courtyard, but also from the unknowns of war.

Hallan turned, and I followed his eyes to the Sky Elves hovering overhead that I hadn't noticed before. He used his hands to sign to them in their language in case they didn't hear everything my father had said. My mother had taught me a few signs, explaining to me the history of where they had come from. She had said when the Sky Elves would fly, the noise of the wind overpowered the sound of their voices, so they used their hands to communicate from a distance. It was good for times when you needed to be stealthy and silent, too. Eventually, it became a part of their culture. Some chose never to use their voices at all, like Ace. I had always found the idea of speaking with your hands fascinating. The movements were methodical and beautiful in their own nature, different from the way we bent the water and they bent the wind. I had always wondered if the wind howled to them as the water sang to me.

Ace tried to help me be more fluent when we were younger, but their language wasn't something I used daily. If you didn't use it, remembering the signs for everything was difficult. Over time I became inarticulate in signing, and as we grew up and saw each other less, I fell out of practice.

The breeze whirling from their inky feathered wings cooled me in the summer sun. I admired the layered feathers as they lowered themselves from the sky. My silver locks of hair fluttered around my face and over my shoulders as they landed gracefully at the front of the crowd. Male and female Sky Elves dressed in fighting leathers stood firmly, interlocking their hands with more of my people and pulling them into powerful hugs, thanking them for their comradery. The only thing left to do was to prepare for what was coming.

CHAPTER TWO

Night fell quickly as my father and I gathered the women and children elves and fae who weren't fighting. My mother joined the healers. Being a water bender brought healing properties we could use to our advantage during these battles. Before my father became the leader of our people, our ancestors believed women should only use their water bending for healing rather than fighting. My father changed that. He believed anyone who had the abilities to protect themselves should. And my mother believed that all knowledge about the element you bent was powerful against any opponent.

They were both right.

Now male and female fae of Esora could bend, fight, and heal with the gift that Mother Moon blessed us with. Healing wasn't a scapegoat. If a wound didn't get treated fast enough, either by our natural fae abilities or by our bending healing properties, death could still claim us.

Hallan landed next to my father, never missing a step as we strode together along the mountainside.

"Report?" my father asked. Hallan came to report any changes to my father every hour.

"Ember soldiers are patrolling Lintawa Bay, monitoring the skies around the mountains. They've completely shut down the dock markets, so there won't be a way to jump a ship. I snuck around asking questions. Apparently, the Ember soldiers have been there the last few days. This was the Emperor's plan all along, long before the Empress found out and warned us," Hallan replied as we all marched forward.

"Damn the Mother," my father hissed under his breath, holding up a fist to stop the small marching crowd. "What's our next option?"

"We can't fly out of here without being shot down, either by the soldiers on the docks or whatever warships are sailing this way in the waters of Draynua. I say we hide the women and children. I found an abandoned cave on the other side of the mountains. The path seems like it hasn't been traveled for a time. We can hide them there for now."

"What about food and water? Enough to last a few days?" My father peered around the crowd.

"My son is delivering food, water, and bedrolls to the cave with a few other elves."

"Where is your wife?" Father asked, and Hallan huffed a laugh with a shake of his head.

"She's in Heavensreach preparing our people. You know my Kali wouldn't miss out on a fight, Ace either, just like your girl there," he said, dipping his head to me with a wink.

My father ran a hand down his face. "Right . . . What does that say about us as fathers when our children enjoy the hunt?" he joked.

"It means we taught them to not be prey." Hallan slapped a heavy hand down on my father's shoulders. "I'd bet our kids take down more men than we do. We're not as young as we used to be, brother," Hallan poked fun.

"Maybe you're not. I'm still in my prime," he said with a defiant smirk as he waved his hand in front of us. "Lead the way."

We walked for hours into the night, sweat beading down my back from the muggy heat. The moon and stars blanketed the sky above the treetops. I hadn't slept or had dinner. My feet ached from the constant pace as we walked along the mountainside to get to the secluded cave. I weaved a drop of water through my fingers, under and over each finger before it skated back over my knuckles, to keep my mind off of the dull ache in my heels and in my stomach. It worked because when I finally stopped, we had made it to the cave.

The mountain's gaping hole was set deep into its side off of the overgrown path, like Hallan had said. You would have to walk right up to it or you would miss it. A cool breeze flowed out of the cave leading underground, causing a chill to creep over my skin. The hairs on my neck stood as if eyes were piercing my back. The ground shifted from soil to stone as we walked inside. Now I knew why Hallan had said to bring bedrolls. A few elves were unpacking while my father and Hallan were lost in a conversation.

"Hey stranger, you need any help?" I asked, and one elf cocked his head to the side to peer over at me. His mirrored gaze met mine. His dark-brown hair was half pulled up away from his strong stubbled jaw line while a tight braid rested in front of one of his extended pointed ears. Three gold cuffs accented the braid as three long feathers were woven into the hair that was tucked behind his ear. Thicker, loose strands framed his face. He looked nothing short of beautiful as he stood from his crouch with smokey ebony wings draped behind him. Elves never let their wings touch the ground unless they were sick or defeated. And I couldn't see this man being either of those things as he walked toward me. His taut muscles flexed beneath his leathers. He stood in front of me but never said a word.

"Ah, I see you found Ace," Hallan spoke up from behind me, walking into the cave with my father by his side. Hallan and his son signed back and forth, but the slight movements were so quick I couldn't catch anything significant.

"Ace—" Hallan gestured toward his son. "—still speaks in our mother tongue."

"I remember from when we were younger," I said curiously. It had been a while. "I'll get him to speak one day," I teased, and Ace rolled his eyes at me.

"Our people consider it an honor to use our mother tongue. It takes a strong will to live by it. I lived by it until I met your mouthy father, who was too stubborn to learn to be fluent."

"Hey, I heard that," my father retorted.

"As you should have." Hallan pointed a finger and my father smiled as Ace chuckled under his breath.

I wanted to ask again, but this time in his mother tongue, so I did. I tried. Turning toward him, I mustered the signs my mother had tried to teach me into the forefront of my mind as I asked if he wanted my help. He cocked his head like a bird and pinched his eyebrows in question before he arched one with a confident grin. He lifted his hand, readying a response, but a gust of wind pulsed from his palm and he knocked me on my ass. I leaped back to my feet.

"Mother Moon, what was that for!?" I cursed, glaring daggers at him. He shook his head and with a wave of his hand sent a wisp of wind tapping on Hallan's shoulder to get his attention, who was currently bent at the waist with my father, laughing at me.

"What?" I questioned, growing impatient.

"You challenged him," Hallan spoke up. "That sign was you asking for a duel." He wiped a tear from his eye as he composed himself.

"No, I think he just wanted a reason to knock me down," I said, dusting off. Ace gave me a knowing grin. We had always been competitive growing up. Challenging each other wasn't uncommon. Hallan walked over to me, corrected me, and showed me the signs slower. The sign with both hands meant duel, and the sign with one hand meant help.

"Now try again," Hallan encouraged as he gestured to his son, watching us with a smug smile, and I did. This time, Ace answered with a nod and a silent clap of his hands in praise as he gestured me toward the bedrolls. He tugged me into a quick hug before pulling away

"Old friend." Ace signed more than that, but that was all I picked up on.

"Yeah, I missed you too, you big lug," I said, and he huffed a breath and smiled.

I remembered a time when we were inseparable as kids, but I guessed gaining responsibilities and growing distant was a part of growing up. He laid out beds for the women and children. I helped him and together we gave each woman and child their own space as Hallan and my father started a fire.

The Sky Elves had a tolerance to the cold. Winters in the mountains were devastatingly frigid. Personally, I preferred the warmth as we gathered around the fire to fill our bellies with supper. I peered over at my father, who was sharpening a dagger. I glanced around the fire, searching for something to eat, but I found nothing.

"Pada," I called to him.

"Hmmm?" His tone was low in question as I continued, never looking up from his blade.

"Where is supper?" He peered over at me and smiled.

"A lesson," he said, and I sighed, letting my chin fall to my chest and shoulders sag. Hallan chuckled at my response. Anytime my father was about to school me on the ways of survival, he always started his statement with this. He never missed an opportunity to enlighten me. I didn't want to hear it tonight though. The sun would rise soon, and I was hungry and tired.

"Aw, come on, Eme, you've always been my good sport." He winked at me, but I rolled my eyes at him and he snickered under his breath before growing more serious. "Catch your food. In the middle of a war-torn world, nobody will feed you but yourself," he said as tiny skittering feet passed by my back. My father threw his dagger, killing the plump rat in its tracks.

"See, there's my dinner," he said as he stood, walking over to it. He picked up his blade, gutting and skinning the animal quickly before shoving a stick through it and roasting it over the open fire.

"Do you ever eat anything appetizing?" I asked, scrunching my nose as he ripped his first bite out of the side of his roasted rodent.

"What would you suggest, darling daughter?" he said in between bites. I knew my mother would reprimand him if she were here for talking with a mouth full.

"A hare, maybe? Or some venison? Anything is better than a rat."

"Alright, then go out there and catch what you want, but let's make it more fun since you want to be picky. No bending, and take Ace with you." It wasn't a request.

Ace signed something to his father, and Hallan translated as he placed his own rat over the fire. I hadn't even seen him catch it. I knew the phrase "Sky Elves were as fast as the wind," but I now realized why it was true. Hallan grinned at my shocked expression before continuing.

"He wants to know why he has to go." Hallan hit Ace upside the head. "Because, son, that was an order, not a request, and no bending for you either." He signed and spoke at the same time. Not because Ace couldn't hear, but out of respect for both cultures.

"As a matter of fact," my father chimed in, "let's make it a friendly competition. Whoever returns first wins." My father never failed to make anything more of a challenge.

"What do I win when I return first?" I asked confidently.

Ace huffed under his breath before looking over at me with an arched brow, as if asking me if I seriously thought I would beat him. His eyes narrowed as he probed his tongue into his cheek in frustration when I didn't back down from my claim.

"I'll get you one of those moonstone necklaces you've wanted from the dock markets when all of this is over," my father said and a smile stretched over my features.

I had wanted one for a long time, but being rich in our way of life and not from wealth made it harder to get things from the markets. That necklace cost four furs last I checked, and my father would never waste four furs on something that was of no use to us. The stone represented light, hope, and new beginnings.

"Deal," I said as I stood, peering over at Ace who was signing something along the lines of "stomping me into the dirt" to Hallan. I begged to differ. I believed he underestimated me as most did, and that would be his mistake.

"I wouldn't be too confident, son," he signed as he spoke. "Eme is Orion's daughter. You aren't kids anymore. You both have quite the challenge on your hands." He chuckled at the end of his statement.

My father shook his head and smiled as he took another bite out of his meal. While Hallan distracted Ace with conversation, I darted toward the gaping cave exit, never missing a beat as I disappeared into the tree line. I heard the heartbeat of wings flutter overhead.

"Cheater," I mumbled under my breath. I knew Sky Elves didn't need bending to fly. Their wings were an extension of them. Like a leg or an arm, they used them the same. But it definitely gave him the advantage. He must have stayed close to the treetops to avoid being seen by any Fire Fae. Even so, it was reckless. If they thought for a moment that he was trying to flee Esora, they'd shoot him down.

Once I was far enough away from the cave, I slowed my pace, using my senses to guide me to whatever prey lay in the woods. Listening carefully, I heard the rustle of foliage, either from an animal or Ace had landed close by. The hairs on my neck stood on end as if my senses were acutely aware someone was near. Adrenaline pumped through my veins as I moved between the uneven trees, until I saw him. I crouched quickly, trying to make myself appear small.

The stag stood grazing in a small clearing between some trees. If I could use my bending, this would have already been over, but my father knew I'd never back down from a challenge. We both had always been competitive. From the moment I was born, he tried to teach and challenge me through every milestone. This was just another test.

Movement caught my attention from my peripherals. I cocked my head to the side but was only met with the darkness of the night. I couldn't fight the feeling of gazing eyes on me. Was Ace watching me? I pushed down the feeling. If he was, I was sure he had already seen my dinner up ahead.

This was going to get bloody. I pulled my battle axe from my side, creeping forward to get a good aim on my target before the animal could sense me and run. I hauled my right arm over my shoulder, launching my axe forward with deadly force. The wind whistled as my blade sliced through the air. Ace dropped through the canopy of trees and grabbed my axe by its hilt before landing. One knee hit the ground like a man bowing before a god. He peered over his shoulder at me with a sly grin before trying to use my blade to kill the stag.

I sprinted forward, barreling straight into him before he had the chance to steal my dinner. Or fly away. The deer darted as we wrestled to the ground. Knocking my axe from his grasp, it skittered through the dirt as I pinned him facedown in the soil. He wasn't expecting me to come for him. He flipped me effortlessly onto my back, knocking the air from my lungs with the force.

"Damn the Mother," I cursed as I grunted against his hold. "That was my dinner. Now look what you did," I said as I snaked my hand to the dagger strapped to my thigh, lurching it up to his neck before he realized. He shook his head with a grin. Using his bending, he blew a gust of wind from his mouth so strong it knocked my dagger from my grasp.

"Okay, let's even the field." I felt for the water deep under the soil we lay on and called for it to heed my command. It coursed through the land, emerged through the dirt, and twisted around his ankles. I dipped my head to the side, and he flew off me and hit one of the nearby trees as I stood, brushing myself off. Ace got back to his feet quickly, giving me a mean mug.

"You started it," I said as he signed to me. To my surprise, I understood.

"Now what?" he asked, wiping the dirt off of his sweaty face.

"We eat rat. That stag is long gone. I'm tired, so I'm going back." I turned and walked away before he responded, and a few moments later, he was walking next to me. On the brief journey back, we didn't speak, but my mind kept snagging on the moment I saw something move. If Ace had been in the sky, then what had been in the woods? I tucked it into the back of my mind. I was growing delusional from the lack of sleep. Many creatures lurked at night. I was sure it was just another dinner that had escaped me.

We made it back to the cave the same way we had left: tired and hungry. My father was still sitting up by the fire, waiting for us to return. Hallan lay in his bedroll snoring, already deep into his sleep. My father glanced over his shoulder before shaking his head in disapproval. He turned to us as he stood.

"What did we learn?" he asked, his eyes bouncing between us both.

"That Ace knows how to run off a stag." I huffed, annoyed, pointing my thumb in his direction as he stood next to me giving me a look filled with venom.

"No." My father shook his head with a sigh. "Mai lao kahi," he signed and spoke as he continued, reminding us of our battle cries. *Forever as one.*

"What does that have to do with the lesson, Pada?" I questioned, frustrated, as my belly groaned and my body ached from wrestling the winged buffoon next to me.

"You should have worked together," he spoke to me while signing to Ace, obviously more fluent than Hallan had believed, or maybe he did know. They had been best friends my entire life after all.

"But you sai—" He cut off my rebuttal.

"I know what I said, a contest and whoever returned first won, but there was nothing stopping you both from winning. You could have worked together and walked back in here with your dinner in hand." He paused, glancing between the two of us again. "Together, as one." He emphasized his words to get his point across. "Nobody wins if you're both starving and tired," he continued, and I glanced over at Ace. His eyes had softened from my father's statement of truth.

"Mai lao kahi," he repeated. "Remember, your goals are the same." He graced both of our shoulders with a firm but steady grip before walking past us to his bedroll.

"There are some rats for you both by the fire. Enjoy your dinner." He spoke over his shoulder before lying down to get some sleep.

Ace and I did. We sat there together and let nothing go to waste.

CHAPTER THREE

Bright rays of light shone into the dark mouth of the cave. I rubbed the sleep from my eyes and stretched. The dull ache in my muscles was almost gone after getting rest. By tonight, I'd be completely fine.

I sat up and grabbed my leather boots. I paused, shaking out both of them, making sure no creatures skittered in there through the night thinking they discovered a new home. Luckily, there were none.

I shoved a foot in and laced it before moving to the other, peering around at the women and children. Some still slept, while others were huddled around their fires preparing breakfast and tending to their young. I looked over to Ace's bedroll and found it empty. I stood and strode toward the exit.

My father and Hallan were drinking their morning tea, sharing small talk about any updates with Ember. Hallan had strapped the modest iron kettle to his belt like a crazed tea fiend, next to his multitude of sheathed daggers that also lined his hip. I guessed it was easier than parading back and forth to the campfire inside. It made a smile tug on my lips.

"Any news, Pada?" I asked in between their conversation.

"Your mother is still with the healers. The elders are teaching and preparing everyone. We've successfully moved those who aren't fighting here, hoping to keep them safer. Ace and a few other elves are delivering the last bit of supplies before we head back to our village."

"Any change to the Ember soldiers at the docks?" I asked, and Hallan huffed a breath.

"Skies above," he cursed, "you are your father's daughter." Hallan laughed, but my father had a look of pride in his eyes as he beamed at me then looked back to Hallan. It sent a warmth fluttering through my chest. I grinned as Hallan continued, "But to answer your question, the docks have stayed the same. We think they're holding back until the rest of their troops arrive."

"Do we know when they'll be here?" I prodded further.

"Based on when we got the letter, they could be here as early as tomorrow morning." His features grew stoney. "At the latest, the day after. We don't know for sure when Ember left to come here or which port they took off from." He paused a moment, looking off into the distance as if he could see the warships sailing the seas.

"But we have elves posted along the mountaintops, scouting for Ember. We should be thankful for the Empress's warning or they would have blindsided us."

He grabbed a cup sitting on the small stone ledge along the cave side, tilted the kettle to pour some warm tea into it, and offered it to me. I took it, turning to my father.

"When will we be heading back home to prepare our village for what's coming?" I said before taking a sip. It bloomed on my tongue. It was a creamy and sweet tea full of heady flavors. Cinnamon and spicy cloves that I had never tasted before coated my mouth. On the second sip, I took down the whole thing.

"We'll be leaving shortly," my father spoke up after finishing his drink. I grabbed for the kettle to pour some more, but Hallan smacked my hand away.

"It's iron, you dolt! And where's your manners?" He spat, and I rolled my eyes. Fae had a weakness to iron, unlike the elves, but that wouldn't stop me from getting more. It was a small kettle, I could handle it long enough to pour another drink.

"Since when are you my ima?" I questioned, and he smirked, taking my cup and giving me some more. "What is this stuff?"

"It's the tea of Heavensreach. We call it pojo. Twice a year it blooms in the mountains. It's delicious, isn't it?"

"Yes, the best I've ever tasted." I hummed as I drank more of it.

"I'll have Ace bring you some, but be mindful. It won't bloom again until the heavy winter," he suggested, eyeing me as I took down my second glass.

"I'll save it for a special occasion," I said, setting my cup down with a smirk, but he gave me a look that told me he didn't believe me.

"When will Ace be done?" I asked and got a grin from both of them.

"Why do you ask?" Hallan winked at me.

"No, it's not like that. Don't be getting ideas," I said to both of them. Surely they had talked about joining our families somehow. Two leaders—best friends, one with a son and one with a daughter. It was too obvious. I shook my head at them again as they snickered to themselves like two boys rather than two grown men.

"I want him to teach me how to sign fluently." I was determined to learn, not just for the benefits of knowing another language, but I was confident it would come in handy with the army sailing Draynua to get to our shores.

"I'm sure Ace would love that." Hallan gave me a joyful smile. "I'll have him meet you back at your village, ready to teach with your tea in hand."

"Thank you, and thanks for the tea," I said as my father placed a gentle grip on my shoulder.

"We should get back." He whistled for a bird. While holding out his arm, one landed on him. He tied a quick note to its leg before sending it off. My father spoke as I turned toward our home.

"I'm letting your mother know we're heading back so she doesn't worry herself sick." When our people left for long journeys or hunting trips, we would use birds to send letters back and forth to check in on each other. Most societies in Osparia used birds to communicate.

"Hallan, keep me updated," my father said over his shoulder.

"Will do," Hallan responded as we started our trek back home.

CHAPTER FOUR

The only things I wanted upon returning home was a bath, fresh clothes, something to eat other than plump cave rats, and to relax from what was happening in the world around me. I hadn't bathed since before my father and I trained. The braids throughout my matted hair pinned it away from my eyes, but loose strands of silver always got loose and framed my face.

My father and I walked up to our small cottage home, and he opened the door for me. As we walked inside, my mother looked up from whatever vegetables she was chopping. The clank of the knife she was using hit the table as she rushed to us to pull us into her warm embrace.

"How is everyone in the caves?"

"They are well. They have supplies and will stay there until this is over." My father rubbed soothing strokes down both of my mother's arms. I could tell she had gotten little sleep. Her bright-green eyes were darker with lingering shadows under them.

"How are the healers doing in their studies?" My father changed the subject.

"Good. Willow taught me some new tricks this morning to pass down to the younger ones. I've been grateful to have an elder healer to teach me her ways."

My father pulled my mother into another tight hug. She rested her head on his chest as he left a gentle kiss against her temple.

"I missed you." My mother's voice was quiet. "Both of you." She tugged aside my father to pull me into her arms. I squeezed her and took in her calming scent. Lavender and minty sage. She always centered me, giving me a moment of serenity in a world that was no longer peaceful.

"I missed you too, Ima," I said, drawing away with a faint smile, "but I really need a bath." She laughed as my father lifted an arm to smell himself. His brow pinched as he got a whiff.

"I'm next after you, so hurry up," he said as he walked over to the table, throwing some of the chopped bits of food into his mouth and pulling out the chair to take a seat while filling his plate.

"Are you sure you don't want to eat first? I made supper?" My mother eyed me, knowing we were gone a whole day without her cooking.

"I'll eat when I get back, Ima. It shouldn't take long," I said while walking over to the ladder that led to my loft. On either side of the main room, we each had our own small loft bedroom. Mine was on the right and my parents were on the left. The wood creaked under my weight as I climbed into my small space to grab some fresh clothes and soap before leaping down to head toward the front door.

"Stay alert," my father said, nodding to me before ripping into a bite of bread.

"I know, Pada." I rolled my eyes at his constant coaching and he threw a fresh piece of bread at me. Catching it, I smirked at him and walked out the door with a mouth full of the buttery roll.

I chucked my boots off to the side. The warm soil and soft foliage crunched under my bare feet as the evening sat in. I glanced around, making sure there weren't any others at the river where we bathed before I pulled my clothes off, letting them pool at my feet. I stepped out of them. The cool breeze pebbled my skin as I approached the water. I dipped my toe in, feeling its warmth before walking out into the slow, coursing river.

My head fell back, and I soaked my hair as I ran my fingers through it, gently pulling out the braids. I grabbed my soap and scrubbed my skin before washing my hair and face. Something tugged at one of my legs, making me jump. I stopped, glancing around the water circling me before I peered up at the tree line, but when I saw them, it was too late.

Four boys from the village bent the water around my ankles from where they stood on the shoreline, dragging me under the watery depths of the river. I wielded the surrounding water the best I could, but it wasn't enough against four others commanding it to do something else.

It swirled around me, trapping me. My nose burned as my lungs screamed for air. I gathered all my strength and tried again, creating a divide between me and the belly of the river. I gasped for breath and pulled my legs into the small pocket I had created for myself. The water surrounding me raged like the caps at sea, barreling its white horses into me as I struggled to keep it divided from me and the stream's graveled floor. And then it halted. The waters calmed. I released the barrier around me as I kicked off the river's bottom and broke through the surface, gasping for air.

The boys that had always bullied me were gone. Being a girl and the future leader of our village often got me terrorized by the men that felt intimidated by a woman in power. And it didn't help that I looked different. My father and mother constantly told me I was a gift from the Mother and we had ancestors who had silver hair, so it ran in the family line, but it certainly didn't stop people from taking notice of my different appearance.

I circled quickly, looking for them, but found nothing. Wings met with dark shoulder-length hair and a big ego were standing on the shoreline waving me over to him. *Ace.*

I swam over from the deep but didn't go any farther as the water lapped at my breasts.

"What all did you see?" I asked, and he signed something, but when I gave him a look of confusion, he shook his head and pointed to the tall trees. The four guys dangled in the distance as they tried to get untangled from the branches. I huffed out a laugh, and when I looked back at Ace, he was smiling at his accomplishment as he waved me over to the shore again.

"Turn around. I'm not getting out with you looking at me." He rolled his eyes with a smirk and turned away from me, leaving me with the sight of his folded wings like those on the back of a bird. I felt my cheeks heat. My tormentors would see me bare if I rose any farther out of the water.

Ace noticed my hesitation and peeked over his shoulder, seeing me looking in that direction. He turned toward me, walking into the river fully clothed until he stood next to me. He gave me his back as he faced the men he blasted into the trees. Water trickled off his smokey black feathers as he stretched out his wings, using them to cover my nudity from their view.

Once I was fully covered, he nodded for me to walk to the shoreline. He matched my stride as he side-stepped until we were on the bank. He never peeked over his shoulder. I gathered my clothes and dressed quickly.

When I was finished, I reached up and grazed my hand down one of his wings to tell him I was done. He shuddered from the touch as he draped his wings back down his back and turned to me.

"Sorry, I didn't mean to startle you." I paused. "They're beautiful." I could've sworn I saw him blush as he pulled me along to walk back up to the village. "Wait." I stopped him. "Thank you." I shook my head and tried to wield my hands with what little knowledge I had of his language and signed it to him, regardless if he could hear me. I wanted him to see my gratitude and my respect for him.

"Anytime," he signed as he urged us along again. His muscles shifted under the wet fabric clinging to them as he walked in front of me. All Sky Elves were built like the mountains they dwelled on. They had to be to wield the wings on their backs. I cleared my throat, not letting my thoughts wander that way about Ace. He was a friend, nothing more, but I couldn't deny he was attractive.

I followed him through the array of trees until we were weaving through the small cottage homes of my village. He approached my home and walked in, not cleaning up, he trudged in muddy water and dirt and I could see my mother's scowl through the window. I laughed as he apologized and sauntered back out with a notepad and quill to write with.

"What are you doing?"

He didn't respond to my prodding. Instead, he handed me the notepad a moment after he had scribbled something on it. It was

39

letters, the alphabet. I looked over at him as he held up his hand with one sign and then pointed to the first letter on the page. I mimicked him as we kept walking. He was teaching me the basics of signs first before moving on to more advanced things. It made sense. If I knew the letters, I could tell him anything I needed to by spelling it out.

I tapped his shoulder and tried my best to recall some signs my mother had taught me as he kept walking.

"Where are we going?" I signed, and his lips tugged on their sides as he nodded his approval for getting the words right. He pointed beyond the trees in the distance, between the mountains and the waters of Draynua. I couldn't place what he was pointing at until his arm wrapped around my waist and he launched us into the skies in that direction.

I squealed as my feet dangled far from the ground below. He bobbed and weaved around the tops of the trees. The powerful breeze dried my wet hair and his clothes as he flew toward the mountainside. I clung to him as I glanced down below, seeing some of the fae scurry around our village like ants from this distance. He gave me a gentle squeeze as if to tell me everything was okay, but that didn't stop the terror of falling to my death if he dropped me.

After a few moments, he gently sailed through the skies. The adrenaline subsided, and I took in the flight's beauty. The ocean in the distance flowed against the sands of Esora, the last of the sun's rays graced me with its warmth over the jutted peaks of Heavensreach, and the nightoak trees stretched their rising crowns, drinking in the last of the sunshine as we braided through them. I fanned out my arms and embraced the summer's wind through my hair. I peered over my shoulder at Ace, who was taking in my reaction to my first time flying with him. A grin planted on his face.

He lowered me onto an overhang on the mountainside overlooking the waters of Draynua. I felt as if I were in a realm between my world and his. I could see where the pillowy clouds brushed against the mountainside so close I could almost touch them, while the nightoaks swayed gently down below. The clouds, sky, and ocean stretched out before me, blending into one as far as I could see. It was beautiful. I couldn't imagine what the view was like on top of Heavensreach. This was only a taste.

The gentle flap of Ace's wings pulled me from my trance as he landed next to me, draping them comfortably on his back before turning to me, scribbling something on the notepad and handing it to me.

Let's begin was written on the paper and we both sat down and let our feet dangle off the cliffside as he taught me the language of his people.

We ran out of paper hours ago. Ace resorted to using a stick and spelled everything out in the dirt under our feet. My head hurt from the amount of information he had given me, from the alphabet to the number of signs that he felt were important to know for the time being with the uncertainty of war. I understood we needed to be able to communicate since he didn't speak or if we needed to be silent in the face of an enemy. Knowing the language of the Sky Elves could benefit us if we could communicate without them knowing. *But what about if we were separated?* I thought to myself before voicing my question with my hands.

"What if we get separated? How will I communicate with you then?"

"We need a call." He glanced out to the blanket of stars lining the great expanse in front of us before turning to me again. "I know, just scream my name." He winked at me and I snorted out a laugh, nudging him off the cliff with my arm. He fell a beat before I saw his wings and crossed arms with a scowl.

"I could've died."

I rolled my eyes, and he joined in on the cackle. "No, something discreet. Try again."

He sat back down and peered over at me before bringing his hands up to his face, blowing out a birdsong whistle. It was loud as it echoed through the treetops. I mimicked him. My first whistle was pitiful compared to his. After he showed me a few more times, I eventually got it down. I still had a lot to learn with my signing, but I knew enough to carry on a conversation and I had the whistle down for us to call each other if we were in the face of danger.

I yawned, feeling the weight of the day as Ace stood, offering me a flight back home.

CHAPTER FIVE

I jolted awake to the sound of the front door creaking on its hinges before it blew off them. Turning over, I watched my father leap down from his loft wearing only his trousers with a sword in hand, landing gracefully on steady feet, his knees bent to absorb the impact.

He raised his sword, ready to strike, until he heard the figure in the shadows release a shuddering breath. My father paused. He lowered his sword as he scrambled to find a lantern, lighting it. We were all met with Hallan's soot-covered face. His eyes leaked with tears as he tried to catch his breath.

"Damn," my father cursed as Hallan fell forward. My father lunged, catching his body before he collapsed on the ground. I leapt down from my loft as my father hauled his limp body onto the wooden table. My mother rushed over, her hands illuminating with a faint glow. A thin sheen of water coated her hands as she wielded it to heal his injuries.

"Hallan, what happened?" My mother's voice was soft and soothing as Hallan choked on a sob.

I walked over to him, peering down. His body was covered in minor burns, and they had singed his wings. Some of his feathers drifted onto the floor. The smell of burnt feathers wafted through our home. It reminded me of the smell of burnt hair.

"She killed them," Hallan whispered. "She killed all of them," he cried out as he rolled his head back, squeezing his eyes shut as if trying to forget the memory of what he saw.

"Hallan." My father grabbed his shoulders. "Talk to me. What happened?"

"Valla, the Princess of Ember . . ." He paused, lifting his glossy eyes to my father's. "She killed the women and children in the cave." He choked on his words as tears streamed down his face again. "Kali—" His voice broke on the name of his beloved mate. My mother gasped, knowing her dear friend met her end. Her eyes welled with tears as her shoulders sagged forward.

"She fought so hard . . . ."

I could feel his pain. It was palpable. The loss of losing his love and so many others radiated through his words. "The men posted along her side tried to fight them off but they didn't make it either. The Princess is leading her father's armies. No one saw them until it was too late . . ." He wailed as he told us about losing the women and children of Heavensreach, his mate, wife, and mother to his child perishing along with them, leaving nothing but stained ashes against the stone walls in the shapes of wings of those lost to the flames and smoke while trying to flee. "I was too late . . ." A few moments passed as he tried to compose himself again.

"They knew . . . They knew where they were as if they had been watching us the entire time." He trembled as my mother continued healing the worst of his wounds. Her shoulders quaked as she listened to him confess the tragedy. She and my father had known so many that were lost. My father's face was grave. The planes of it were hard in the faint lantern light of our cottage. His jaw ticked as his anger spiked.

He grabbed for his leathers and weapons. He gripped Hallan by his forearm and pulled him up from the table. My mother had healed him up nicely, but he would need more sessions if he wanted to get rid of the scars left behind.

"Mai lao kahi." My father placed his forehead against Hallan's in a comforting embrace. "We will fight for those we've lost, brother."

Hallan ran a hand down his stained face.

"Wait," I finally spoke. "Where is Ace?" My eyes searched Hallan's, pleading with his stare to find that Ace had not met the same fate.

"He's gathering the rest of the men on the mountain. They'll be down here any minute."

"Where is Valla?" my father asked.

"She retreated after the battle. Both sides suffered losses."

"She had to have had someone watching us, gathering intel on our movements as we made decisions." My father ran a hand through his hair. "Damn the Mother, damn it all!" he shouted. Turning, he rushed to the counter and swiped his hand down it; the food canisters flew and clanked loudly as their contents leaked onto the floor.

My mother jerked from the sudden sound. She wrapped her arms around herself as the chill of death lingered in the air. She cupped her hands around her face as she cried, and my father's features softened.

"Ivy," my father whispered her name as he approached, gently wrapping her in his strong arms. "It'll be alright, love." He tightened his embrace but we could all feel the tension in the room. Nothing was okay. Women and children, Sky Elves and fae were here one moment and gone the next. Letting that thought sink into my mind and claw at the depths of my heart made tears swell and stream down my face. What being could close their eyes every night knowing what they had done to those innocent women and children and feel any kind of peace?

From the rumors over the years, we had heard about the Princess of Ember being a villainous creature. But this was beyond that. She was the type of person our people told scary stories about around the campfire. The ones that stuck with you in your nightmares. The type of person who had no regard for the pain of others. She took pleasure in every wound she inflicted.

"I'm scared," my mother finally said, "for all of us." She peered over the three of us in the room with cloudy eyes.

I walked over to them and my father welcomed me into their embrace. He held us for what felt like an eternity, and I did everything in my power to memorize the moment, burning it into my memory and engraving it into my heart and soul. What lay ahead was unknown. The only thing I knew for certain was that whatever we faced, we would do it together.

CHAPTER SIX

My father and Hallan prepared. Seeing them work together under the stresses of war and grief highlighted why they were leaders for their people. Dark clouds loomed over every fae through the villages of Esora to the elves dwelling on the tallest peak of Heavensreach. The men gathered, their faces focused. No man or woman would grieve until the battle was over. Unfathomable numbers of fae and elves lined up together. Swords glinted as wings splayed through the crowds.

Some practiced their battle routines on the sidelines, while others sharpened their weapons. I peered over the faces, looking for someone in particular, but came up empty. That was when I remembered our call to each other. I gathered the air in my lungs and pushed a birdsong whistle through my hands, echoing it through the trees, but nothing answered me. Seeing Hallan with my father, I walked over to him as he fastened freshly-edged daggers across his chest.

"Hallan, I haven't seen Ace. Do you know where he is? I'm beginning to worry."

He dropped his eyes from mine, exhaling deeply.

"He's probably on one of Heavensreach's cliffs. His mother always loved the views." His voice was gruff as he cleared the emotion from his throat.

"I'll find him, thank you," I said as I turned to walk in the direction of the cliff we were on only yesterday. The things that could happen within a day would never cease to amaze me. Happy memories had gone sad. I never knew I could feel cold and empty in the middle of summer.

"Eme," my father called to me, "I don't want you to be alone. Take someone with you."

"I'll be fine, Pada, and I won't be alone. I'll be with Ace."

"Eme." My father's voice was demanding. His eyes were filled with so much love, concern, and fear.

"Pada, I know. You have taught me everything I know. I'll be alright." I gave him a small smile, hoping to give him some reassurance, but it didn't diminish the worry in his features.

"Hurry back," he commanded with a nod in the direction I was heading, and I darted through the trees in a sprint.

Within minutes of running through the plethora of trees and foliage, I peered up through the canopy to see the cliff I had trained on with Ace. I couldn't see anything at first, but upon closer inspection, I saw two leathered boots dangling from the large jutted-out piece of land.

"Ace," I yelled, getting no response or movement from his hands. I gathered the breath in my lungs to let out a whistle. Still nothing. I sighed under my breath as I approached the rough stone surface of the mountain and found a good place to put my hands and feet and started scaling it. The stone was cool under my calloused grip. I had rock climbed before, but never as high as he was. I used all my strength and climbed one reach at a time, every movement getting me closer to him.

My blood pumped faster through my veins the higher I got.

Don't look down.

I repeated that mantra over and over in my head as I kept my eyes focused on where I placed my hands and feet. Sweat beaded my brow as my hair whipped and clung around my damp face. The growing altitude made the wind whirl and gust harder against me.

"Ace," I panted, glancing up at him, "the least you could do is—" My foot slipped from the rock it had found purchase on. It crumbled under my weight as I held on for dear life. My other hand slipped and my body jerked from the sudden stop. I heard my shoulder pop as I gripped the mountainside with one arm. Throbbing pain shot through my body. The skin across my palm tore open from the rough stone. With a pained grunt, I tried to pull myself back to the mountainside, but the stone gave way, falling out from under my grip.

I went weightless. Fear slithered through the pit of my gut as I fell. A scream worked its way up my throat before the sound of wings and powerful arms encompassed me. My heartbeat pounded in my ears and my adrenaline subsided as Ace sat me down where he was sitting moments ago. He landed, but his gaze never met mine.

"I didn't ask for you to come here." His features were hard. Every muscle in his body was taut.

"Well, you're stuck with me now because I will not be doing that again." I glanced down the mountain, trying to ease the tension. His jaw ticked. He definitely didn't find my words to be easing anything.

"Leave me alone." He signed with a growl radiating from his chest. "Go home while you still can."

"No." I spoke calmly. He would not scare me off in his time of grief when he didn't want to admit he needed someone the most.

"Leave." He crowded me against the stone. His signing was direct, his facial expression letting me know that if he spoke, his voice would be filled with guttural venom.

"I won't." My voice was barely above a whisper as I looked up at his pained face. His chest heaved as he turned away from me in anger and released a roar that echoed through the mountains and a gust of wind that tore down the surrounding treetops. I watched his back as his shoulders rose and fell with his heavy breaths and his wings sagged. A few moments of tense silence passed before I made my way to him.

I touched his shoulder, gently tugging him to face me. His eyes stayed pinned on the dirt at my feet as he turned. I wrapped my arms around him tightly. The throbbing pain in my shoulder barked at the movement, but I didn't care. I felt him rest his head in the crook of my neck as he accepted my embrace. After a few beats of my heart, he wrapped his arms around me and squeezed. I felt the warmth of his tears on my neck.

I hissed as Ace wrapped my bleeding hand. It would heal within a few hours with my fae healing, or I could heal it now if I had some water on me, but I didn't. And I didn't need to waste any more energy by trying to wield it from afar.

"I'm sorry," Ace signed. "I should've come to you."

"Don't be." I shook my head at him. "I can't imagine what you're going through, but I can promise you I'll be here." I gave him a reassuring smile.

"Thank you." He offered his hand to help me stand as he stretched out his wings. "We should—" He stopped signing as he looked out toward the open expanse. The bright orange glow reminded me of the sun rising over the ocean. But it wasn't the sunrise. It was the burning glow of Ember fae soldiers creating a wave of fire in the distance, almost as if they were waving a flag to let everyone know they had arrived. I could already feel the heat gathering around me as the flames grew taller. My eyes widened and my lips parted as Ace reached out his hand.

"Time to go . . ." My voice trailed off as he gathered me into his arms and launched us into the skies, toward the direction of our front lines.

CHAPTER SEVEN

T he heat radiated from the glowing flames as we grew closer to our people waiting on the ground below. My father and Hallan were on the front line together, and a cascade of faces glared at Ace and I as he landed and gently placed my feet on the soil. My father was next to me within three long, quick strides, pulling me into his embrace. I buried my head in his chest.

"Where have you been?" He let out a shaky breath. "I was so worried about you." I had never heard fear in my father's tone before, but it encompassed every word. He feared what was coming, and it made my heart plummet to my gut. My father had never been afraid of anything in his life. He was always strong, and fierce, and my rock anytime I needed him to be. He was the reason I grew up to be everything that I am, and he'd be there to watch everything that I would become after we made it through this. I was sure of it.

Hallan stood still as stone when he laid eyes on his son. They glared at each other solemnly as the silence of loss stretched between them. The pain on both of their faces grew as they approached each other. Hallan released a shuddering breath as he pulled his son into a firm embrace with tear-lined eyes. He held him close, as if letting him go would mean losing him too. It seemed to be the first time they were seeing each other since Kali's death. They had lost so much within a night. We all had. But there was no time to mourn. We would mourn once the battle was done.

"Where's Ima?" I asked as I peered over at the faces closest to us.

"She fell back with the rest of the healers, where she's needed most." He released me. "If you hurry, you can get there and back before we march."

I nodded and gave him one last quick hug before darting around the crowd of warriors. I glanced back at Ace and signed to him I'd be right back before I disappeared through the array of bodies. Pushing my way through sweaty warriors and slick leather armor, eventually I made it to the back, through the trees, where the healers were preparing themselves.

Something seemed off. All of them were standing still. Tears lined their eyes, as if we had already lost this battle. Our people always had a strong will, so I didn't understand why the healers all seemed to be in a somber trance.

Seeing my mother, I ran and barreled into her, wrapping my arms around her, breathing her in. I had seen how much could change within a night, and I didn't know what was going to happen from this moment forward. I savored her warmth before she stepped from my hold and cupped my face in her hands. Tears were already streaming down her face. I smelled the metallic tang of blood and glanced down at her, looking for wounds.

"I'm okay, Eme," she said with a shaky, reassuring smile.

"Why are you bleeding? What happened, Ima?" I asked, seeing a small, leaking wound on her side, staining her clothes. I tried to tend to her, but she brought my attention back up to her face.

"Listen to me, Eme." Her voice was a tremored whisper. "I love you, with every fiber of my being . . ."

"Ima, you're scaring me. What's wrong?"

Her eyes shook as she studied me closely, and then she suddenly realized something. She removed a hand from my face and moved it to her side. The movement was so faint as she told me something.

"Poison," she signed with her hand. It was so minuscule anyone else would have missed it. Especially if they didn't know the language. It was a warning.

I kept my features calm, but I was falling apart internally as the dread of what had happened dawned on me. Ember poisoned our healers.

Being a healer meant you had the ability to restore others, finding their injury from the inside out, using your power to mend them. Most water benders had the means to heal themselves, but to use your abilities on others was a unique gift entirely that took time to master. Even if our people had the potential to heal, if they were bleeding out or weak, doing so would be impossible if they had already expended their energy in battle. And it wouldn't matter if they tried if a moment later there was a sword waiting at their necks or fire aimed at their hearts.

I tried to steady my breathing, but the looming shadow of what was happening was waiting within the trees. Ember was here, somewhere, and I had interrupted their plans. The wave of fire was a taunt, like a flag waving us in the direction they wanted us to go, herding us like animals, thinking that was where the attack was forming. All the while they planted poison in our healers and were ambushing us from behind.

My mother brought her hand back up to my face, bringing me out of my thoughts as her lip trembled.

"Eme, go back to the front with your pada. We have everything taken care of back here," she tried to reassure me again, but in reality, her eyes were telling me to run, to get help. I shook my head, but her eyes grew stern at my resistance. Ember was here, but my mother was only thinking of my safety.

"Now, Eme," she commanded.

"Ima—" My voice cracked.

"No, my love, do not say goodbye to me." She sniffled, pulling me into a tight hug, placing a gentle kiss atop my head. "I want you to know that whatever happens, do not let this world take away your light."

"Enough with the sap." A vile cackle followed the man's statement as he came out from behind the trees. More followed behind him. They were lying in wait, listening within the trees. Some healers were already so weak they lay on the ground or leaned against a tree, their breaths growing more ragged by the minute. All the men wore all black, and some wore masks while others showed their faces proudly. Their uniforms were not the same as Ember's, but I was sure Ember had something to do with this.

"Run, Eme." My mother turned, pulling water up around her, preparing to buy me time to escape. Her legs trembled; her stance was weak. She wouldn't make it.

"Aw, how sweet, but we both know you won't be doing much damage with hemlock coursing through your veins." He flashed a wicked grin as flames ignited, licking up his arms. The men followed his lead, lighting the forest in a faint orange glow. Hemlock wouldn't kill a fae, not in small amounts, but it would make them feel like death. They'd be feeble and sick until their bodies had time to burn off the poison.

"Emelyn, run! Now!" my mother shouted as she launched sharp daggers of water in their direction. Panic and adrenaline flooded my senses.

"What about you!?" I cried.

"I said go!" she screamed while pumping the last of her strength into her bending, keeping the Fire Fae surrounding the woods away as they blocked her blows. My vision grew blurry with tears as fear sunk into my gut.

"Now, Emelyn!"

Panic took root in my chest. I ran, or stumbled, my way through the forest. I couldn't remember; everything became cloudy. Screams echoed behind me, my mother's screams. There wasn't enough air in my lungs. My heart hammered in my ears. Goose flesh slivered down my spine. Pain shot through my chest. Sweat dotted my brow even though I was trembling from the chill that had crept over my skin. Arms wrapped around me as my vision came back into focus. I saw black feathers and muscled arms. He shook me back to my senses. His eyes looked me over for any wounds before they met mine. My heart shattered, but I remained emotionless, numb from what was happening. He held me close for a moment before he palmed my face with one of his hands.

"I got worried and came looking for you, what happened?" Ace signed with his free hand as my trembling slowed.

"Ima . . . ," I croaked, and his eyes widened in recognition. He yanked me back into his grip. His warmth pieced my shattered soul back together, if only for that moment. I felt relief in the comfort of his hold. Shock overtook me. I didn't have time to mourn. I'd mourn when this was over.

"We have to go . . ." I sounded muffled against his hard chest. "Ember is using hemlock to weaken us. They ambushed the healers."

He released me and we darted to the front lines. The march had already started. My father and Hallan were at the front. I wasn't close enough to warn him about what had happened when a figure approached. Part of me wondered if he already knew about Ima. Could he feel it? Was it something he felt inside himself, or had Ima blocked him out during her final moments? Or was it like a change in his world? I didn't know the workings of being mated. I had only heard the stories.

A woman stood in the distance. She wore a cocky grin on her face, hip cocked to the side with black pants and leather boots laced up to her knees. Her hair was as dark as onyx and her eyes were so golden, they almost looked red, like the flames she wielded danced behind them. She was devastatingly beautiful. Power radiated from her presence. An army of men lay in wait for her command.

"Hand over the chosen, and no one has to get hurt," she called out loud enough for all to hear.

"You mean like the women and children you killed!" Hallan shouted, rage lacing his tone.

"Oh right." She tsked. "I meant to say, no one *else* has to get hurt." She winked at Hallan, a proud smile stretched across her wicked face like she had won a prize for the death of innocents. This was a game to her, one that she enjoyed playing.

He launched forward, but my father grabbed him, holding him back. The men standing behind her had fire blazing from their fists the moment Hallan moved in her direction.

"You're fucking dead, Valla! You hear me? Dead!" Hallan's voice boomed through the silence of the battlefield, his grief palatable in the air. I now knew why this woman was the Princess of Ember, the leader of her empire's army, known for her ruthless wrath and apathetic nature.

"Why are you here, Orion?" Valla questioned, disregarding Hallan all together. "I'm not here for you or your people. I'm here for the elves."

"Anyone willing to kill innocents that walks on the soil of my homelands is labeled an enemy in my eyes. My people chose to stand against you with the elves."

"Then you shall fall with them." Her statement wasn't a warning; it was a promise. She would watch the world burn until only she was left.

CHAPTER EIGHT

The Fire Fae marched forward, and I rushed to the front where my father was.

"Pada!" I yelled as I pushed through until Ace wrapped an arm around my waist and launched us over the remaining crowd of soldiers to get to my father and Hallan.

"What is it? What's wrong?" His voice was ragged as I tried to explain.

"They ambushed us. They took down the healers with hemlock and Ima . . ." My voice fell and my father's eyes went dark, as if I had just extinguished the last of his light and hope. He nodded, looking into the distance. I thought I had confirmed what he already knew. He cocked his head toward Valla and she grinned at us, a knowing expression on her face as we put together her plan all along. She never intended for a fair battle. Valla had snaked her way into our land and placed her men strategically like a game of cat and mouse. She aligned her tile pieces carefully, right under our noses.

"You poisoned them." My father spoke up to Valla. She unsheathed her sword, revealing the glinting light-brown, straw-colored liquid dripping from it.

"I don't play by rules, Orion. I make my own."

My father snapped. He lunged forward, blade drawn in one hand, water whipping from the other, with Hallan by his side. Everyone moved at a breakneck speed before flames, water, and wind clashed like a tidal wave of power. Flames licked up the trees, and the forceful winds blew down the weak ones, turning them into nothing but ash.

Shouts and booming orders echoed from all directions as my father yelled, "Watch the blades! Try to disarm them!"

"Turn their weapons on them!" Hallan shouted from the sky.

I didn't even see him take flight. Flames barreled at the winged men soaring above the battlefield. Some fell, the smell of burning hair and flesh tainting the air. Swords clanked, arrows surged through the winds, missing their original targets. The elves used their powerful winds to shoot the arrows back at the Fire Fae, making them lurch before falling to the ground. After a few moments, they started convulsing and puking from the poison in their veins before one of our people finished them off.

Valla, Hallan and my father battled, their movements full of grace and power. How Valla was managing to take on both of them was unbelievable. She blocked their blows with raging fire and poisoned metal. Her movements were full of complete control. She blocked and weaved and fought with a precise lethal venom. It took years to master a skill of that level, something she had to have obsessively trained herself to do over the years. Maybe she trained with her father, too. The thought made me realize how different things could be when you had a loving role model compared to one full of hatred. A part of me pitied her, but only for a moment.

Ace and I were back to back on the ground as we fought the Fire Fae who charged us. I sunk my battle axe into a man's shoulder. His flames fizzled out, and he toppled to my feet. I shifted, withdrawing my blade as I readied for the next attack, when a searing, hot pain shot through my side. The man on the ground tried to attack me with his flames again in the last moments of his life. I kicked him away, finishing the job I had started, before moving on.

Rain poured down from the sky. I wasn't sure if it was from the gods, mother nature, or from the power of my people. Fire sizzled and hissed against the cold water. Wind gusted around me, making my dripping hair plaster to my face. I tasted the salt from sweat and iron from blood with every swing of my arm as it painted the wind and water.

I glanced over my shoulder back to my father and Hallan, but something was wrong. My vision grew hazy, time seemed to slow, and sounds were distorting. At the same time my eyes found my father's, it was as if he knew something was amiss. He hesitated, and Valla took advantage of her opportunity.

"Orion!" Hallan's voice boomed across the land as he soared through the air, pushing my father out of the way, taking Valla's sword through his heart. I watched as it played out in front of me so slowly, as if time had stood still. I felt my legs go weak. My father yelled for me as a bright white light stretched across the land in front of me. Was this the end? The light was erratic and crazed as it moved in every direction before it shot through my father from Valla's hand.

Lightning. She had mastered beyond her fire.

I screamed as my father's body fell to the ground. I moved toward him but my legs failed me as I collapsed into the mud. Everything was on fire, but no flames caressed my skin. Every ragged breath made my side flare in pain. Ace's dirty face came into view. I felt him cradle my head as he tried to sign to me.

"Where are you hurt?" he signed, but my limbs felt too heavy to sign anything back. I tried to speak, but it came out more like a murmur.

"Side," was all I could manage. Without hesitation, Ace ripped apart my burnt leather vest and found a leaking wound. The man from before didn't just burn me, he had stabbed me. Ace growled under his breath.

"Stay with me, Eme," he signed to me, but his hand grew more foggy by the minute. Ace grunted as he tried to stand, and I thought it was from trying to lift me until he dropped me to the ground and turned toward an enemy. A dagger's hilt protruded out of his back, directly between his wings. The fae man ignited his arms in flames. He looked as if he were staggering, already injured, but that could have been my vision playing tricks on me, making the world feel like it was shifting around me.

A burst of air blasted from Ace, but it didn't harm me. The icy wind made my skin pebble against my soaked clothes. The fae that attacked barreled away like a leaf, falling away from the trees in autumn.

I watched as Ace created a dome of wind around us. He turned back, cradling me quickly against his chest, before he launched us into the raging elements around us.

Fire, wind, and water came from all directions. Pouring rain pelted against my skin like shards of glass as I felt my body drift in and out. Ace roared across the land, and as if his people knew the call, they took flight, but it was too late to retreat.

Bright light, red flames, and darkness consumed the sky as Ace's wings carried us through the devastation of Valla's wrath. Suddenly, we weren't in the storm of chaos anymore. The surrounding air stilled. The world had gone quiet, as if Ace had become an island of calm amid stormy seas.

We had made it out. Ace's flying staggered as he glided through the empty skies. Dark spots clouded my vision. Unconsciousness was calling to me. I did everything I could to keep my eyes open as Ace swayed toward the ground below. His breathing grew ragged and uneven as my head lay limp against his chest. His flying faltered. I felt weightless before I met the cold earth below, and then nothing.

CHAPTER NINE

My arms dangled as I swayed and bobbed to the rhythm of someone walking. Blood pounded behind my temples as I came to my senses. I knew being awake wouldn't last long. My body still felt like it was on fire and tingling all over. A rigid shoulder dug into my hips as I was bent at the waist, hanging over a man, staring at the moving ground below. I suspected it was Ace until I saw Ace being dragged through the dirt behind me. He was on his back, his wings drooped and outstretched to the sides of him. Panic laced in my chest, constricting my heart. I didn't know if he was dead or alive. I assumed the latter since someone had thought to drag him along with us.

I tried to move my arm. Tried to get it to do anything, but the most I could move was a twitch of my finger. I was helpless, being carried by a stranger through the woods with no one coming to my rescue. I tried to listen to my surroundings. I didn't hear the sounds of war anymore. Black spots began clouding my vision again as I drifted off.

I faded in and out of consciousness.

I saw Ace's wings leave a trail in the loose soil behind us. Then a man wearing black. The warmth of a palm resting against my cheek. And then I was laid down. Everything was out of focus when I opened my eyes; it made my head ache. I closed them again, letting them rest as someone lifted my shirt and touched my bandaged side. I winced before I heard the elderly woman's voice cut in.

"I'll take care of that. You need to go," she said, and he lowered my shirt. I remembered seeing the old woman as the man left. I never got to see his face, never heard his voice. He had tended to my wounds and saved Ace and me. I didn't even know his name. I felt safe in the woman's presence. Wherever he had taken us, it wasn't out of malice. I wanted to thank him, but I was too weak to move as his figure grew smaller in the distance until he disappeared into the shadows.

I jolted awake to the sun beaming through the trees. Ace lay in a cot a few feet away; his chest rose and fell gently in his sleep. I tried to sit up, but every muscle in my body barked from the movement. Everything hurt. My head pounded from the morning's light. My mouth was so dry. A skin of water lay next to the bed. Grabbing it, I smelt it before bringing it to my mouth. I drank every drop of the cool liquid. Some leaked from the sides of my lips, but I didn't care. I touched my side, now dressed in clean bandages, as my mind processed what had happened. My first thought was my father.

I leaped out of bed, ignoring the throbbing pain that came with every movement. I stumbled out of the small hut-like home we were in. Now that I was getting a good look at it, it wasn't much. It was tucked away in the woods. The elderly woman was nowhere to be seen.

Wind chimes, trinkets, and colorful bottles dangled from the nearby branches. Chime trees surrounded the home.

Some believed the trinkets helped with healing; others made wind chimes to represent stories about our history and our people. There was a narrow path through the branches of trees leading to the small hut. Soothing, clinking sounds resonated on the light breeze. One in particular called for my attention as I ran my fingers over the smooth painted glass. A sun and moon were one as stars hung and danced below them, twirling in the breeze. It reminded me of a bedtime story my mother and father had told me growing up.

I forced it aside as I ducked under the low-hanging branches. The smell of ash and fire was easy to follow, even though I didn't know where I was. I tried to sprint toward it, but my limbs were still too weak. The poison slowed me down as my body continued to burn through what remained of it.

I pressed my legs to go, to move through the grimly quiet woods. My lungs burned, my side stretched in pain with every long stride of my legs, my head pounded loudly in my ears, but I pushed on. The trees changed, charred from fire. Some lay on their sides, some nothing but a long pile of soot. Until the land became open and nothing remained but cinder and dust where the battle had taken place.

A sound came from my left and water whipped around my arm, preparing to strike on instinct. But when I turned, the elderly woman stood there. She had brown skin and peppered gray hair braided to the side, revealing her pointed fae ears, and lines crowded around her mouth and eyes from age as she held up her hands.

"Hello, Emelyn. I need you to come with me," she muttered, eyeing the water swirling around my arm as I let it fall to the ground. She turned to walk away, and I followed her.

"Where are you taking me?" I glanced around at the remains of the battle and tears pricked behind my eyes. Valla had left nothing. "I need to find my pada. Who are you? Why did you help me?"

"I'm taking you to him." Her voice didn't sound reassuring as she went on. "I am—was—your mother's teacher. I am one of the elder Kumai. We stayed behind during the battle." My mother had mentioned her teacher's name was Willow.

"Where is everyone else?"

She didn't respond. I saw bodies on the ground in front of us a short distance away, answering my own question, and I stopped in my tracks. They had covered some with a blanket or tarp of some kind. There was no rise and fall from their chests; they were already gone. Others lay still breathing, barely. I looked at Willow, her warm brown eyes filled with so much sorrow, but she broke my gaze, unable to meet my eyes as a single tear fell from her.

"Where is my father . . . ?" My voice shook on every word, my body numb.

She couldn't speak. She only pointed me toward a bedroll, where I assumed he was lying. It took me a moment to build up the courage to walk over there. My eyes grew blurry with tears as I pushed past Willow. Every step made the lump in my throat grow, clogging the airway to my lungs.

I slumped to my knees next to him. His breathing was slow and raspy. I palmed his cheek, pushing his brown hair away from his face.

"Pada . . . ," I whispered, and he opened his glossy, tired eyes to look at me. A small smile pulled on his dry lips.

"There's my girl." His voice was weak, but he struggled to sound like himself. I laid my hand on his chest. A thin sheen of water glowed under my palm as I tried to see the damage. Tried to heal him. He placed his hand over mine. "Eme . . . It's too late for that."

"No." Tears streamed down my face. "Don't say that."

"I asked Willow to keep me here long enough to see you one last time."

I sobbed at his admission.

"Pada, please . . . I can't lose you too."

He grunted as he moved his trembling hand and reached into his bedroll, pulling out a moonstone necklace. My shoulders quaked. I gave him a sad smile as another sob escaped me.

"This cost me eight skins," he continued with a light chuckle, as if he wasn't telling me goodbye. He took his hand away from mine on his chest and tugged a pendant loose from under his clothes to show me he wore a matching one. I collapsed against him and wrapped my arms around him in a tight hug. He held me weakly, as it was all he could muster. He groaned in pain but continued to do it anyway. As I parted from him, he put the necklace around my neck and wiped away my stained cheeks. "I will always be with you."

I kept his palm against my cheek, savoring the warmth of him before he tugged it free.

"Now I need you to go with Willow."

"No . . . I'm not leaving you."

"Eme, I—"

"No, I'm staying. You will not leave this world alone."

He was too weak to argue. I lay down next to him on my uninjured side and curled my arm under my head as a pillow. He cradled my hand on his chest, and I watched it faintly rise and fall. Willow walked up on his other side, and now that I was getting a better look at her, she looked exhausted. Both her tawny hands glowed as she examined him, and he grabbed one of her wrists.

"It's okay, Willow, thank you. You can let me go now, I'm ready to be with my wife." His words clawed and shredded my already broken heart, reminding me that I had not only lost my mother, but now I would lose him too. Willow had been keeping him alive with her abilities this whole time. I could tell she had gotten no sleep with the amount of people in bedrolls she and the handful of other elders were tending to. Her brow scrunched in pain at the thought of letting a patient go.

A leader, friend, and father.

She shook her head and looked away before looking at me. "It won't be long without me tending to him."

I nodded at her truth. My heart sank to the pits of my gut. A numbness fell over me as I laid my head back down and peered over at my father on his deathbed. I studied each curve, every line of his appearance, branding all the memories we had together in my heart to be sure I'd never forget them and everything that he was—and still is to me.

My tears slipped freely as my face remained fierce. Willow used a damp rag and dabbed his face one last time as she murmured under her breath.

"For eternity, let the light of the Mother find you and bring you peace on your next journey. Your fight in this life is finished . . . Until we meet again," she said her last goodbye as we did to those who left us before she stood to tend to her other patients.

My father's eyes remained closed. He looked at peace. I lightly squeezed his hand, and he returned the action. I lay there for what felt like hours, but it was only a few more moments until his fingers went slack and his chest fell for the last time. I scooted close to him. Tears blurred my vision as I buried my head into his chest and let all my broken pieces fall away until I was nothing but a hollow shell.

He was gone, and I was nothing short of lost.

CHAPTER TEN

I watched Ace, in his silent grief, have a moment with his father. Hallan had died on the battlefield, and I had so much empathy. He didn't get the chance to say goodbye to either of his parents like I had.

When he had finally woken up, he came and found me clinging to my pada and had to pull me away from him. Willow took his body to clean him up and prepare him for his send off along with a few others that didn't make it through the day. Watching her work nestled a seed of pride in my chest. Willow had been tending to our people along with the other elders from dusk till dawn. Despite her advanced age, she kept up with everyone's needs. Being fae, we had endless lives unless killed. I couldn't help but think of all the things she knew, all the stories she could tell. Now I understood why my mother had such deep respect for her.

I succumbed to nothingness. It took over like the poison that had coursed through my veins. This pain was nothing compared to being hurt in battle or cut down in training. It was like losing your soul, but you had to continue living without it, becoming an empty husk that breathes and eats. Being alive was like the rivers. Their currents never stopped moving. Life wasn't going to give me pause, regardless of the darkness that came with it. We had to keep going, keep breathing, living . . . for all of those who no longer could.

Wounded fae, battered and burned, limped or stumbled, trying to prepare for the sendoff of their loved ones. Some bodies had made it, though not very many. Others had already turned to ashes in the wind, becoming one with the battlegrounds of Esora, or had fallen away to the waters of Draynua.

So many people were lost. I hadn't seen one Sky Elf since the battle. Not a single feather, and I wondered if Ace was the last of his kind. That was who Ember had come for to begin with. Did they annihilate an entire race? For what? The thought made rage rise within me. Ace stood, turned to me, and didn't sign a word; he only pulled me into a tight hug.

"You scared me. I woke up in some strange woman's hut and you were nowhere to be found," he signed as he pulled away.

"I'm sorry. I felt you were safe where you were." My heart sank as I peered around at the destruction. "I just had to get here." A ball formed in my throat and I had to fight to swallow it down before I fell apart again.

"I need a drink," Ace signed, and I handed him my skin, but he shook his head at me. "Not that kind of drink." He cocked his head to the side with a bemused look. "Have you ever drunk alcohol?" he questioned, and I answered truthfully.

"No, I haven't. My mother would kill me." The words hit me as soon as they left my lips and fluttered off my hands. She was gone too . . .

My father used to invite his friends over to drink and play Tile. It was a strategic game they would play and bet with skins or coppers. Sometimes they'd even bet each other's chores for the week. He would drink with them and always seemed to enjoy the time with his allies and friends, but my mother never drank and would have strangled my father with the water she wielded if he let me do it or even offered it.

I pushed it out of my mind for now as Ace continued, "I'm sure they would understand this once . . ." He released a heavy breath. "After the send off, let's get some air, away from all of this." He gestured around and I nodded in agreement.

Willow walked up to us from behind and handed Ace a large cloak. "You need this. Ember left because they thought they had destroyed your kind. They scoured Esora for hours when they overtook the battle but came up empty. They left before Emelyn got here. Hide your wings if you're walking around the public in the light of day, and I'd only fly at night if you absolutely have to."

Ace's eyes were wide with adversity. His wings were a symbol of pride for his people and now, after losing them, Willow was asking him to conceal a piece of who he was. He stood there, shoulders tensed, going ramrod straight as if rooted to the ground. So still.

"Ace . . ." I touched his arm, pulling him from his trance. He had nothing to say as his brow knitted together in grief and anger. His features grew cold as he snatched the hooded cloak.

"I'm sorry, dear." Willow's brown eyes were stern but full of empathy. She placed her small hand on his shoulder before stepping away.

"Willow," I called to her. "Who saved us?" I asked, and she turned toward us again.

"I did. Your father was so worried about you. He wouldn't let go until he was sure you were safe." Her voice was soothing, comforting, like a mother's touch.

"No, I mean, who brought us to you? Who was that man?"

"A traveler in the woods found you near my home. Luckily, I was heading back for more supplies or I would've missed him."

"What was his name?" I asked.

"I didn't catch it. He left quickly, dear." She gave me a warm smile. "I'm glad you both are okay." She touched my cheek gently, and it reminded me of the touch from when I was drugged by the poison. I felt foolish for thinking it was the stranger that had tended to me. Everything I remembered was so blurred and distorted. I didn't know how long I had been out or how far the man had dragged us along before reaching Willow, but I was thankful he had helped us.

The moon loomed high in the night sky as Ace and I stood on the sandy beaches overlooking the calm waters of Draynua. Its light made the white sands look silver. Soft waves lapped against the shore as we prepared the small boats. We had spent the rest of the evening bending and molding them for those that had passed. As I whipped my water through the wood, I couldn't help the burning behind my eyes while I prepared the boat that I would soon lay my father to rest in and shoot an arrow through in remembrance of him. It was all too much to process and, for a moment, I just wanted the emotions to stop.

Ace and I helped one another as we pushed the boats out into the open waters. Willow said a prayer, hoping those lost would find their way into the next life. Fae lit their arrows as they passed by the campfire. All of us had lost someone. Ace and I were two of the last to light our arrows as we stood in a line with everyone else. All of us pinched the bowstring, pulling it past our faces as we aimed.

"Mai lao kahi." I choked over my words. "Until we meet again." I released my hold on the taut string and the flaming arrow hit its mark as the boat slowly engulfed in flames. The heavy fog resting over the waters in the distance made the flames on every boat look soft, almost beautiful. They were like a light showing you the way in the dark, until they slowly dissipated to nothing and the only thing left were the soft cries of the injured left here to live on.

I decided in that moment that I would live for my parents and for all those who were lost that day, and we would rebuild from the cinders and dust left behind from this battle. But for now, I just wanted to take a moment to forget the ache in my heart.

Ace had flown us to the cliff's edge. He wasn't doing well with the idea of not using his wings or hiding them. My legs dangled over the side as I looked down at the free fall below, where I had almost become a puddle of blood and bone before.

It was the middle of the night and we had both sent off our parents to the next life, along with having already drunk two bottles of something called gin. I learned that not only did the Sky Elves have excellent tea, they apparently knew how to drink, too. Fermenting juniper berries and grain had a way of taking the edge off. At this point, my vision was blurred, and I was sure my signing was just as slurred as my speech. But Ace still went back up to Heavensreach to grab more.

Earlier, when he flew up the mountain for the first time, he told me how there was nothing left. The flames had consumed everything. Apparently, the only reason he was able to get alcohol was because Hallan had a stash in a small cave along the mountainside. You had to fly to get to it.

I smiled at the thought. It sounded like him. I imagined my father probably teased him about it, but then they would meet there for gin and Tile. I could see it so clearly in my mind's eye. After clearing my throat, I tore the image out of my head and became a mess of tears. We were supposed to be giving ourselves a small reprieve, a moment to just try to forget the bad and remember the good, and I didn't want to ruin it by sitting in a pool of my own tears.

I rubbed my hand down my face as Ace landed with two more bottles and a small bag of something. I stood, stumbling over to where he landed.

"What's that?" I asked, but my words came out slowly.

"My dad's Pojo stash." He tried handing me the bag and another bottle of gin.

"No, keep it, but I'll take the gin," I said, without signing, as I didn't know if I could anymore.

"No, he'd want you to have it. He told me about how much you loved it before he sent me to give you some." His hand movements were slow and I smiled at his truth and took the bag from him. That day seemed so long ago when I drank Pojo with Hallan the morning we left the cave to go back home. So much had changed.

I turned toward the mountain, stumbling toward the wall with Ace, when I tripped over my own feet. His arm caught around my waist before I fell headfirst into the rough stone. Instead, we tumbled over beside the wall, falling next to each other in the cold soil. His mirrored gaze met mine, his arm still draped around my waist. His hard chest was at my front while the mountain sat at my back.

I gave myself one breath before deciding to fuse his mouth against mine. I brought my hand up to cup his lightly-stubbled cheek. He didn't kiss me back at first, and right before I was about to pull away, he tucked me against his hard chest and deepened our kiss. I just wanted to feel something. Anything other than the misery of what had happened in our lives. He was my distraction, and I was his.

I tasted the pale liquor that lingered on his breath as our tongues intertwined. A groan rumbled in his chest that made a moan escape me. Tears stained my cheeks as I tried to forget. I only wanted to think of him.

As quickly as his lips were on mine, they were gone. Ace stood, fumbling for his full bottle of gin. He took a long swig before turning to me with glossed-over, tear-lined eyes.

"This isn't you, or me, Eme." He blew out a breath. "This is two people experiencing a loss and trying to run from it." He shook his head as if trying to reel his thoughts back in line through the drunken stupor. "Tell me . . . If we hadn't gone to war, would you have kissed me? Would you have wanted me in that way?" he asked, and I didn't have an answer. Ace was attractive, yes, beautiful even. But he was my father's best friend's son . . . We grew up together. I believed our fathers had always wanted us to end up together, but if we truly felt the same, it would've happened long before this.

"You're right. I-I'm sorry." My voice cracked over my words, and Ace pulled me to my feet, steadying me.

"Why? There's nothing to apologize for."

"I don't-I can't lose anyone else. I don't know if I'll survive."

"I'm not going anywhere." His face was serious. Sure. His hands were firm.

"You can't promise me that." I wiped my damp face for what felt like the hundredth time in the last day. I wasn't sure how many more tears I could shed.

"I promise that as long as there is air in my lungs and a beat in my heart, that I will be here, we will be here, together."

"Mai lao kahi," I whispered with a sad smile on my face, and he held out his hand and nodded his agreement. I took it, grabbing his forearm, and he pulled me to him, placing his forehead against mine before wrapping me into a tight hug. He brought me the comfort of knowing I wasn't going through this alone, and I hoped I brought him that same feeling.

Ace had always been there with no reservation or reward. He wanted to be. From the moment our fathers introduced us, we had been close. Life would get in the way when it came to seeing or spending time with one another, but the affinity between us was always there.

"Come on, we need to find a place to sleep," I said, pulling away. My buzz was wearing off and a slight ache had started behind my temples. I walked over to the edge and waited for Ace as I picked up my bag and bottle of gin. "You coming?"

"Shouldn't I be asking you that since I'm the one with the wings?"

I smiled.

"I trust you." I said it with a wink as I stepped off the side of the cliff's edge. Ace jolted, leaping over the edge, falling with me before catching me in midair.

"You're crazy," he signed with one hand, and I let out a chuckle. Maybe my body was still reeling from the alcohol.

Within a few minutes, Ace was landing in my village at the bottom of the mountain. Not much remained. Some cottages were still standing, but they were badly charred and I wasn't sure how much would be salvageable. Some survivors had made little camps around the village as a temporary fix until they could start rebuilding their homes. Others stayed at the beaches where the elders were tending to the rest that had survived.

"You want me to go?" he signed.

"No . . . wait here. I'll only be a minute." He nodded, and I walked forward to where my home sat. The door was gone, the walls blackened and barely standing. The lofts had collapsed. I moved to the one my mother and father used. I remembered my mother always kept a chest with leftover blankets and bedrolls. Hoping the fire hadn't gotten to it, I dug through the debris. I found it lying on its side, covered in soot. Somehow it had made it. I yanked it free from where it was, taking the axe from my side and knocking the clasp loose from how it had congealed together. The chest creaked open, and I grabbed the few blankets that were in there. They smelt like wood smoke but it was better than sleeping on the forest floor.

I peered around my childhood home, reminiscing about every first I had here: every night my father told me bedtime stories, every time my mother had taught me something new, and every training session my father gave me in the main room before my mother would kick us outside.

I gave myself this moment, just one. For the faultless child who grew into the young woman she was now. The girl who thought her people, her parents, and everyone she had ever loved would still be here. I guessed it was a naïve thought to think peace would last. Maybe my heart wasn't cut out for this heartless world.

I held the blankets tight against my chest, as if they would bring the warmth back to the void left inside me. They didn't. I straightened myself, not glancing back, releasing the part of me that believed in a peaceful life behind on a shaky breath that vibrated through my chest like angry thunder before a storm. I said goodbye to everything that was and accepted everything that we were now as I walked back out of my ruined home.

Ace waited patiently by the training grounds my father and I had used every morning.

"Here." I handed him a blanket and kept walking past him. He didn't push me to talk about it, just like I hadn't pushed him at Heavensreach. He followed until I found a small clearing that felt like a pleasant spot to camp. I tossed the blanket on the ground, lay down, and tucked my arm under my head for a pillow, and Ace did the same. There was no talking or signing. As the alcohol wore off, we lay there staring at one another in silence, until my eyes grew heavy and I drifted to sleep.

CHAPTER ELEVEN

I awoke to stiff hands touching my side. I lurched for my axe
and bent water, aiming it toward whoever was touching me.
They blocked it as I rubbed my sore eyes, my sight still fuzzy,
as Willow came into focus. My temples throbbed. My guess was
from alcohol being fun while drinking it, but not fun afterward.

"What are you both doing here?" she questioned.

"We found a place to sleep. What does it look like?" My tone
was full of attitude, but I was still exhausted, nauseous, and I
could hear my heartbeat in my head.

"Why didn't you come back to my home?" Her tone remained
level, calm.

"Didn't think we had an invitation just because you tended to
our wounds."

"Well, come on then." She nodded toward her home and didn't wait to see if we were coming as she started hobbling away. The brain fog from the night before was affecting me because I gaped at her with a knitted brow, unmoving, trying to figure out if she was being serious.

Her dress swished at her ankles, her long gray hair weaved into a loose braid down her back. She glanced over her shoulder, "Are you coming? Because I'm tired, my patience is running a little thin, and I need to know how many mouths to feed tonight." Willow spoke with a quick tongue and a soft heart. She didn't have to give us anything, but she was offering us her home, her food, her attention.

Ace was still sound asleep. I saw his boots lying on the ground between us and grabbed one, chunking it at his chest. He woke up with a grunt, looking around, confused. It was early morning, and I knew we had gone to bed late. He squinted up at me while I gathered up my blanket.

"Come on," I said as I stood, walking in Willow's direction.

Ace stumbled to get himself together quickly before he caught up to us.

"What is going on?" he signed lazily, still trying to get his body to function after the night of drinking we had.

"You're both coming with me."

I didn't have to speak; Willow did, without even glancing over her shoulder. It was like she had eyes in the back of her head and she knew what Ace was asking. "I could use some extra hands around, and the company," she continued as we followed closely behind her.

We stayed quiet during the walk to Willow's small hut of a home. She laced the trail leading to her dwelling with decorative trinkets, crystals, and wind chimes dangling from the surrounding tree limbs. The gentle noise of clanking wood and chimes brought me comfort in a way. Maybe because this was the last place that I felt safe.

She moved to the side, waving for us to come in. Walking through the threshold, I could tell the place wasn't big enough for the three of us, but Willow had done her best to make us feel more at home. The cots that she treated us on still sat in the back of the room with fresh sheets. There were no lofts. It was one room, and a small kitchen sat to the right, along with a little wooden table and chairs.

To the left sat a divider, a living wall full of different plants and vines growing from it like a vertical garden. She had a small conservatory in her home in case someone needed tending to. The house smelled of wet earth and flora. Everything from spices to remedy plants and herbs hung from and climbed the small wall. I assumed her bed was behind it.

Ace went to touch some of the bigger leaves dangling from the wall.

"Careful, some of those bite back," Willow said, glancing over her shoulder with a wink. "You'll be itching for a week, but don't worry. You'll learn more about those while you're with me."

Ace and I gawked at her as she sauntered around her small kitchen gathering the ingredients she needed to make something to eat.

"We'll have chores to do, too. We'll cast the nets for fish and sell skins for coin at the dock markets. I'm sure you could work on your healing skills too, Eme." She paused, placing the handful of things she had gathered on the wooden table before she signed to Ace. "And don't think I forgot about you." She smiled, and Ace ran a hand down his face as he tried to process everything.

"How do you know sign?" he questioned. Willow eyed him with a scowl as if he had insulted her.

"When you've been around as long as I have, child, you learn a thing or two."

"How long is that?" I asked curiously.

"Long enough." She nodded toward the things on the table. "Now, help me get these things out to the fire so we can eat and get some work done today."

We did as we were told. My headache subsided through the day's labor after some water and a meal.

We made breakfast. Cast the nets. Had a lesson on plants. And by the evening, we were huddled around the fire outside, preparing dinner and getting ready for the day's end. Willow's cooking was immaculate. I guessed having knowledge of herbs and spices, along with many other things, had done her well in knowing how to cook a good meal. The woman could make plain oats taste good, and she had just this morning.

The calm wind flowed through the trees. The chimes and clanking sounds echoed gently when the same wind chime from before caught my attention: the sun and moon twisting with one another.

"Willow?" I called for her attention.

"Hmmm, child?" she asked, looking up from whatever fur she was weaving as we sat around the fire together.

Ace kept tossing daggers into a nearby tree and would use his air bending to bring them back to himself.

"What is all this?" I gestured to all the things dangling from the nearby trees.

"They all hold a story or have a purpose. Would you like to learn about them?" she asked, and I nodded, peering up at them all. "Alright, how about you pick one and I'll tell you a story about it?" She gave me a smile, and all I wanted was to hear her knowledge.

"What about that one?" I pointed to the sun and the moon and she shook her head as if she knew I was going to suggest it.

"I think most of us know that story. But it's one of my favorites, so I'd love to tell it. The wind chime represents the god of the sun and the goddess of the moon. Long before our time, they waged war. Neither won nor lost, neither stronger than the other, but equals. Always tugging and pulling against one another. After centuries of endless strife, the moon became tired and dull, and the sun took notice, giving her a sliver of his light to bring back her glow. The exchange created peace among them, and they blessed Osparia. Their power coated the land, soaking into the ground and becoming one with the people that dwelled here, blessing us with the abilities we have today." She paused, glaring at Ace. "Which is why we should use our abilities for more important things rather than knife throwing and being too lazy to get up and go get it."

The knife fell midair at her statement and Ace rubbed his neck as his face bloomed with embarrassment. I giggled under my breath, but felt a pang of sadness fill my heart. My mother would use those same words on me. The loss of her filled me suddenly, unexpectedly.

I missed my ima and pada more than words could describe. Willow had been the only thing keeping me grounded. I felt she did the same for Ace, too, after everything that happened. She kept us busy in our ways of life and hadn't mentioned who we all lost the day Ember came. Willow's voice brought me out of my thoughts.

"How about you pick something every day, and I'll tell you its story every night before bed." She gave me a warm smile, leaning over to give my hand a gentle squeeze as if she could hear the thoughts in my head.

"Sounds like a plan," I said, returning the gesture.

And she did.

Over the following months, Ace and I learned of plants, tending wounds, cooking delicious foods, and trading at the dock markets, and every night, after our long days of labor and learning, she would tell us a story. Some were about dragons and other fantastical beasts that roamed our world, while others were lessons on those we should fear.

Willow had become our anchor in our storm of grief, and I was thankful.

CHAPTER TWELVE

STRANGER

The old woman in the woods hadn't lost her touch like I would have thought. When she saw me lugging Emelyn and her winged companion along, she assumed I was doing them harm, turning them in to Valla. But in reality, I was saving them.

I watched as Emelyn fell from the sky in the arms of the elf, and I slipped away from the battle. Fear consumed me. My need to get to her made my legs act, and my boots had sunk into the bloody soil. That was the only reason I had come to begin with. I didn't want to be a part of this war, but it was too late for that.

They had been poisoned and were covered in blood and sweat. I quickly treated them as best as I could before dragging them through the forest. I had to get them far enough away, and that was when I was met by a familiar elderly woman with a temper.

I rubbed at my side where she had knocked me on my ass from the force of her bending. The water soaked me and she left my side black and blue from the impact. It would heal soon, but she was powerful, given her age. I'd give her that.

I stood on the ship's deck, peering out over the dark waters of Draynua. Not a sliver of land was in sight as we changed course, heading back to Iron Isle Harbor. I watched the waves crest and bob in the never-ending distance of blues as the sky met the sea. The ocean breeze misted my face, and a sense of calm enveloped me.

I had done it; I had found her. And I would do everything in my power to keep her safe, even if it meant staying away.

To be continued...

To find out what happens to Emelyn and Ace, purchase book one of The Osparia Series:

Fate of Water and Wind

ISLANDS OF ASH

AN OSPARIA SERIES NOVELLA

By Lashell Rain

CHAPTER ONE

I had been lying to my people about my whereabouts throughout the day. As a recently marked chieftess, I felt guilty about it. I should be open to them as their protector, but I still hadn't mustered the courage to tell Baron what I was doing. I guessed that didn't make me a dutiful wife either, let alone a leader.

But I realized that the fae warriors of our small piece of the world of Osparia had traditions, customs so instilled within them, they would never find this acceptable. They would never change their ways for the dragons that roamed through the Espien Islands—our islands. Maybe I was the crazy one as I stood in front of one, talking out loud to her as a friend while I mulled over all the thoughts in my mind.

The battle between dragons and warriors had raged on from when I was a babe. Before my time, the fae of our islands only had one view of the dragons—that they were vile bestial creatures that roamed our land and stole our food. Over time, it became a tradition that if you slayed one, they considered you one of the finest warriors, the title being something to be proud of. One of the customs that my people still lived by was simple. When you became of age, you slaughtered a dragon to prove yourself worthy of being titled as a fae warrior. But I had never viewed them as dreadful beasts. If anything, I had seen a reflection of myself through Emeris.

Beyond that simple rule, we had lived peacefully amongst them since times of old. I ran my hand up and down Emeris's rough leather-like skin. The light reflected off of her scales, making her almost look dark purple, although her color was black from a distance. She nudged me with the side of her angular head, and I giggled, smiling up at her. Her bright-yellow eyes met mine, and I admired her fierceness. That was something I needed more of.

"How about one more ride for the day, Ris?" She perked up at my offer, spreading her wings with a purr of excitement before she lowered her colossal frame down to the ground so I could get on her back. I climbed on, and she nudged my leg with her snout to ask if I was ready as she inched toward the edge of the cliff. I patted her neck, letting her know I was, as she spread her wings and dropped over the ledge. Her wings caught the wind, and we were soaring into the clouds of the open blue sky. My smile stretched across my face, and the wind tousled my long braided locks as Emeris's powerful wings took us further out to sea. Once we were far enough away from home, we flew below the clouds and enjoyed the views before grabbing fish from the depths of the ocean and heading back.

My people believed I wandered out into the forest on hunting trips for food or resources to use around our homeland. What they didn't recognize was while I did that, I was riding the dragons they were raised to fear and kill. After several long moments of playing in the clouds, Emeris free fell to the water, so close the talon at the ends of each of her wings skimmed the water. The cool mist on my cheeks made me laugh aloud and splash her back before I noticed it. She was giving me a side glance, and I recognized her playful features.

"You better not." I said it at the same time she dipped down, submerging us under the water. I gripped her neck harder, holding on, and for a few moments, the world went silent as the rushing water flowed over my head. Emeris whipped her fin-like tail once, twice, and then we were breaking the surface of the ocean once more.

The rush of air hitting my wet body and dripping hair sent a shock to my senses. My skin pebbled while Emeris shot back up into the sky. I rubbed her neck, laughing off the adrenaline rush, and her low purr back almost sounded like she was laughing with me. Her head turned, and she glanced at me. I pushed my hair away from my face. The black coal that lined my warm brown eyes smeared against my bronze-toned cheeks as I wiped away the water.

Soaring high, I glanced at the horizon in front of us and spotted something I'd never seen before. At first, I thought it looked like a storm coming in from the distance, but as the large black specks grew clearer in my mind, I wished it were a storm rather than what I was seeing. A small fleet of Ember warships was sailing straight toward the islands.

I pulled up hard on Emeris's neck, launching her back up above the clouds, not wanting to be spotted by the Fire Fae headed toward our home, but it was too late. Large balls of fire shot through the clouds, one after the other. The only thing that kept us from being hit was the way the clouds glowed a faint orange before the flames broke through the bottom.

"Go, Ris, go!" I commanded; her wings beat faster, causing the air to shift the high clouds we were riding across. Emeris moved so fast, the only thing I could hear was the whistling wind in my ears. The minutes seemed like seconds through the panic of my racing heart. Soon I could see our home in the distance, while the ships behind us were long left out in the sea. I let out a shaky breath as Emeris landed atop the same ledge we fell from, and I leaped off her back and buried my head into her chest, wrapping my arms around her neck.

"Are you okay?" I asked, pulling away, dragging one of my hands down her, doing one full lap around her entire body checking for any cuts or burns. She nudged me with her snout, a loving gesture I learned from her from the many months we had spent together. She blew out a puff of smoke in my direction, making me remember she was a dragon and not just my best friend. Her leather-like skin was fireproof, considering she was a beast created to withhold the flames in her chest.

"Hilarious." I rolled my eyes at her, and she nudged me again, almost as if she were trying to thank me for caring. I smiled, but it faded as I realized I had to tell not only Baron but all my people what happened today. And I did not know how they were going to take it.

The Emperor of Ember had wanted to strike the world of Osparia and take it for himself from the moment he sat on the throne. The only thing stopping him was the Peacebringer being alive. If the rumors were true, the Emperor took the vision the soothsayer foretold about the next bringer of peace, and no one could have guessed what he had planned next. His cruel heart had no limits after what happened in Heavensreach.

I wouldn't let my people do anything to Emeris or any dragon. There was a battle far worse sailing upon our horizons.

CHAPTER TWO

As Emeris flew back to the dragon's nest, I bid her farewell. I made my way through the rugged forest terrain; my thigh-high leather boots protected my legs against the overgrowth. I trekked my way back to my village down the small mountainside pass I had made for myself.

The walk back was a sizable distance, considering our island. Out of the many smaller ones surrounding us, ours was the largest. I saw the smoke rising from the campfires and small flute chimneys as the night's dinner was prepared. The aromas of sweet bread and meats filled the air. Some of my people greeted me as I walked by them. Elise waved as she walked hand in hand down the center of our village with her daughter and her mate.

Ravi held his daughter's other hand. Every other step, they swung her in between them. Her feet kicked up the dirt, and her laughter warmed my heart. I gave them a quick smile and nod, but my head barely noted any other greetings as I walked to my cottage home where Baron should be waiting. We made all of our homes from the trees. They were built in rows to accommodate our narrow passageways between cottages, huts, and small shops. My nerves racked through me as I approached my home.

I took a deep breath, tried to calm my racing heart before opening the door, knowing I had to share my secret with him. The door creaked open, and the aroma of fish already cooked and prepared for dinner filled our home. Baron was shirtless, wearing nothing but his trousers. His rippling, muscled figure almost distracted me from what I had come to talk to him about as he turned to peer at me. His long dirty-blond hair fell over his shoulders as his gray eyes met mine. He greeted me with his rugged-faced grin. He stepped toward me, wrapping his powerful arms around me, pulling me into his embrace.

"How was your hunt, my dear?" His deep voice vibrated across my neck as he placed small gentle kisses along my collarbone, making my breath hitch in my throat. I ran my hands up his bare chest, cupping his face. Bringing his eyes back to mine almost made me choke on a sob, and he noticed as I pulled away from him.

"Shay, what's wrong?" His voice filled with loving concern made my heart clench harder against my ribs. I had been keeping secrets from the man I loved with everything in me, my husband, my mate. How could I have let it go so far when he had given me everything?

Baron cupped my cheek, bringing my eyes back to his, growing more unsettled.

"Shay—talk to me."

"There is something I need to tell you." My voice came out weak.

"What is it?" he questioned again.

"I'm scared—" My voice cracked as he pulled me back to him again, holding me against his warm chest. Hearing the faint beat of his heart sent warmth through our connection, calming me.

"Whatever it is, we can face it together," he whispered in my ear.

"I've been lying to you—to everyone," I said, pulling away from his hold.

"About what?" he retorted.

"I never slew the dragon." My voice went quiet.

"That's what you're so worked up about? We can always go together—"

I cut him off before he could finish. "Baron—I don't want to slay the dragons. I won't. The day our people sent me to kill a dragon, instead of killing it—I befriended her." I stumbled over the end of my claim, observing him as understanding showed in his features.

"Her?" His brow furrowed.

"Emeris."

"You named a dragon like it's some pet?!" He dragged his hand through his hair, his voice wavering.

"Baron, please, now is not the time." I tried to get to the point. "Today, while I was riding, I saw something far worse than the dragons; a fleet of warships are heading this way. It's Ember. It looks like they've started the war."

"Riding . . . ?" He ran a hand down his face, taking in everything I'd said.

"I have been dragon-riding since the night they sent me to kill Emeris."

He moved over to the small wooden bench, pulling it from under the table before taking a seat in disbelief. His brow pulled in as his mind reflected over what had been happening without him knowing.

"You've been lying to me this whole time . . ." He looked up at me, his head shaking. "Why?"

"Because you're Baron the Dragon Slayer. I didn't think you'd take the truth very well."

"Shay, I am your mate—your husband—before any other titles. Just because I have killed more than one dragon in my life doesn't change that." I could feel the black clouds growing bigger in my chest, taking up my space to breathe. The guilt of lying to him for so long slowly piled up. My head drooped from my shoulders. Baron was the only fae I knew that had faced over one dragon in his lifetime and won while trying to protect one of the meat traders who traveled to our island. No traders, meat or any other, had come since Ember attacked Heavensreach, and I doubted they would. Ember had taken control of as much as they could after that dark day. Trade to smaller consumers being one, it seemed. They staked a claim with their destructive ways, letting the world know they were waging a war. Soon all the trade markets would be run by their soldiers. The Emperor would slowly infect the land with his rules, his men. Eventually, he'd be monitoring everything and everyone, gaining control over what he could, inch by inch, and destroying anyone who denied him.

I felt Baron's rough fingers grip my chin, pulling my face back up to look at him as he stood in front of me.

"Hey, all we can do is focus on what's coming. Ember has chosen war. We should count your riding as a blessing for warning us before they've reached our shores." He walked away, grabbed his shirt, and pulled it over his head, slowly strapping his leathered armor back on as he spoke. "Besides, if this dragon is our ally, as you say, then we should be grateful. Going against Fire Fae soldiers being fae with no bending is no simple task; maybe this Emeris will help us evacuate if things go amiss." The understanding and maturity of the man I had been blessed to be mated to would never cease to amaze me.

I placed my hand over his chest plate, pulling his attention back to me. His face leaned into mine as one of his hands slid up my back, grasping the hair at the nape of my neck. He pulled me into a passionate kiss. A tear escaped from the emotions clawing at my chest, and he used his other hand to wipe it away before pulling me back again.

"Later." He released a heavy breath, giving me a wink, and I smiled.

"Thank you," I said before he grabbed his sword, sheathing it at his side and walking toward the door of our small cottage-like home. I followed his lead as he stepped back outside, bracing himself as he prepared to warn our people of the war. He walked toward the forest, and I caught up with him.

"Where are you going? Shouldn't we talk to our people first?"

"I think we should go talk to your dragon pet. Our people trust us to protect them. I need to be sure that your friend isn't a threat."

"If people approached you with blades drawn, you wouldn't be friendly either. Don't blame their destructive nature on them. They are creatures trying to protect themselves, just as we are." I paused for a moment, letting him take everything in. "We are more like Emeris than you think." He said nothing, but the expression he gave me was all I needed to see. He understood, even if he didn't believe it for himself yet.

"Lead the way to Emeris, my dear." He held his hand out in front of him, gesturing for me to go ahead. We followed my forest trail, and he noted the small path I had carved for myself.

"How did I not notice?" he questioned under his breath.

"Notice what?" I asked, glancing back at him over my shoulder.

"You'd leave for hours at a time in the day to go hunt when I've seen you shoot a bird down within seconds of being out in the forest. You're excellent at setting snares, and you've always been one to do things promptly, and yet I still never questioned you about being gone for too long."

"Love can be blinding."

"I should have paid better attention to my wife."

I stopped dead in my tracks and turned around on the trail to face him. "Don't." I placed my hand against his chest, stopping him.

"What?" he responded, looking at his feet.

"Blame yourself for my lies. You couldn't have known. I did my best to cover them because it scared me. I didn't want you to see me differently." Turning away, we walked onward, almost to the craggy cliff where I always met Emeris.

"How did you think I would see you?"

"As a lying, no-good wife." Saying it aloud sent a pang through my chest.

"You went into the forest to slay a dragon and tamed one instead. You're the bravest warrior I've ever met, and I'm grateful to call you mine. Nothing will ever change that, love." My heart rate quickened as flutters floated from my gut to my chest, easing any pain that had rooted there before his kind words. The cliff came into view, and I paused. Turning around, I ran into his hard chest, and he wrapped an arm around my waist.

"Are you sure you're ready for this?" I questioned as my eyes danced over his face.

"I've been training to slay dragons my entire life. You think I fear your pet?" He furrowed his brow with a grin, and I rolled my eyes at his cocky smile before I whistled my signal to her. A moment passed before Emeris flew straight up over the edge of the cliff. Her wingspan blocked the sun's rays, casting shadows down upon us. I watched a slow smile of amazement creep onto Baron's face, and it made me smile up at Emeris with him. She circled in front of us before she came back down and landed on the cliff. She paused, stiffening her posture, making herself appear more threatening. As she looked at Baron, she showed her razor-sharp teeth.

"Easy, Ris, it's okay. He will not hurt you," I said while walking toward her, and Baron grabbed my hand, holding me back out of concern. He didn't understand our friendship. I placed my other hand over his. "It's okay; she's gentle."

"She doesn't look very gentle," he spat, his eyes narrowed at her.

"I'll show you." I stepped up to Emeris's colossal figure, running my hand down her neck. She guided her head down over my shoulder, tucking me into her chest as if she were hugging me, and it brought another smile to my face. She kneeled low to the ground so I could get on her back, and Baron looked at me, confused.

"What are you doing?" he said.

"Come on, don't tell me that Baron, the slayer of beasts, is scared," I teased.

"No, not scared, just . . . concerned," he fumbled, thinking of the right word.

I snickered at him and held out my arm. "Come on, I want to show you." My offer floated between us as he looked at me for a moment, his eyes full of uncertainty. Finally, he took my hand and climbed on Emeris with me. His legs tucked under mine, and he had me sitting in his lap as he wrapped his arms around my hips. My center heated from the feel of him under me, sending a shiver through my limbs.

With our duties to our people helping them run their shops, hunt for food, and train our warriors, Baron and I took advantage of the little time we got to spend together. As young fae mates shortly after our marriage, our people marked us as the Chief and Chieftess of the Espien Islands, but the title came with the work. During the mornings, I helped the townspeople with their things before hunting in the evenings while riding Emeris.

Baron used the few wooden boats we had and checked in on our smaller islands. Few resided there, but he gathered herbs for medicines if needed and took the warriors to train. By the end of the day, most of the time, we were exhausted from the day's labor. Even that hadn't stopped our desire for each other. I was so entranced by all the places our bodies were touching, I hadn't realized that Emeris was leaping from the cliff's edge.

Baron gripped my hips as we glided above the sea, and I had to suppress the heavy sigh of desire that hitched in my throat. His length hardened under my rear as he reached his hand up. He wrapped his calloused fingers around my neck and pulled me back against his muscled chest, whispering in my ear.

"I can smell your need, love." He dipped his other hand into the waist of my pants, sliding two fingers through the wet heat that was waiting for him. I let out a soft moan from his touch. He toyed with my small bulb of nerves between his fingers as he palmed my center before he sunk his fingers into me. I gripped his forearm as I tried to ride his hand. He had already found the spot inside me that made my body go hazy. That needy sensation ignited within me, making a whimper escape me. His groan reverberated in my ear, making me shutter. "We need to calm down or I'm going to take you right here in the sky."

"I . . . I don't think Ris would appreciate that." I stumbled over my words, trying to catch my breath, reel in my thoughts. He didn't release my neck. Instead, he held my head there, his grip tight enough for the excitement to slice through me. As Emeris glided us along, Baron planted small kisses down my jawline before he pulled my head back at an angle to have access to my mouth. Kissing me, his tongue begged for my permission as I opened my mouth to deepen our kiss. A low, gruff growl rumbled from his chest, and the sound alone almost pushed me over the edge. My center clenched for more, but he pulled away, placing his hands back around my waist. He brought his mouth back to the edge of my pointed ear to whisper,

"Later."

"I'm beginning to hate that word," I sneered, disappointment lacing my tone.

And he chuckled, a deep, soft laugh that pulled me back to the reality we would be facing. What if this was the end? What if this was the last time I would hear his soothing laugh? If Ember had started the war, the Emperor wouldn't stop at the Espien Islands; he'd want all of Osparia to be under his control. We'd heard the rumors. Ever since he attacked the mountains of the Sky Elves, extinguishing them from this world, he had a taste of death, and he wanted more. Baron's hands rubbed small circles on my thighs, trying to smooth me.

Even though he couldn't see my face, my stiffened posture must have given away where my thoughts had gone. Being mates didn't help when trying to hide our feelings. If I let down my internal walls, he could feel the depths of my soul, every raw emotion, my thoughts, the sharpest of my edges, and I could feel the same from him. When we discovered we were mates, it was all-consuming. It still was, but now we had better control over it. Mostly. As my mind wondered through my sultry cravings, a small smile tugged at my full lips.

"Look," he said, pulling me out of my thoughts. He used one of his hands to point forward, and I tapped Emeris to bring her to a stop. The line of figures in the distance was all we could see, but that was as close as I was going to get after what happened last time. I could tell it was the same fleet of warships from earlier today. I glanced up over my shoulder at Baron as he shook his head with a knowing expression on his face. The war was here, and we were Embers' next mark.

CHAPTER THREE

E meris landed back home, and Baron leapt down. I could see his mind racing as he offered me his hand to help me down.

"We must prepare, ready our warriors, set the traps. We will fight at daybreak." I took his hand, watching the worry grow in his eyes. We had never been to war. We lived here amongst the dragons and with our customs peacefully for as long as I could remember. Even as a child, the stories told around the fire were tales of peace and filled with togetherness. Now? It seemed Osparia was falling into the hands of the Fire Fae of Ember. I turned to Emeris, running my hand down her snout.

"I'll call for you when we're ready." She nudged me before lifting her head, blowing a gentle puff of smoke that made a smile hint at my lips. Her smokey ash and milkweed rose scent engulfed me, reminding me of our home. The intoxicating smell was sweet and heavy with warmth. It was almost like I could feel the ashes of ancient times surrounding me. Soothing my nerves. It was like Emeris held the embodiment of our homelands in the pits of her chest. I gave her one last pat as she took off into the skies.

We rushed back to camp. Sunset was approaching quickly, and we didn't want to lose any more sunlight than we already had. Through the last few years of hearing the rumors of Ember starting the war, we had been preparing for this day. We knew being the closest islands to them, we'd be one of the first places they'd try to conquer as their own. We'd never had to use deadly fae traps or be trained so fiercely as warriors until the rumors of war spread, making us push ourselves harder than before. Baron had always been one to be prepared for anything, Ember included. As a leader, it was a part of our job to be ready.

Baron called for the warning bell to be rung, and slowly, all of our people gathered around: wives, children, elders, fathers, warriors, all fae, but none of us had the gift of bending the elements like others did. The islands had become a small haven for nonbenders, although I was sure plenty lived around Osparia. This was a home for many of them.

Seeing them gather around made my heart clench against my ribs. How were we going to keep everyone safe? The thought of knowing that some faces I saw would no longer be here tomorrow almost made the tears burning behind my eyes slip down my cheeks.

I took a deep breath to gather my composure. The last thing I wanted to do was cause panic, but Ember took down the Sky Elves at Heavensreach. They destroyed a powerful race of elves within a matter of a few days. No warning. No compassion for life. Their fire rained down relentlessly. It scorched the skies in the distance red for days after they left, almost like the flames that took the blood of the innocent stained the clouds.

Knowing these heartless ones were coming to our shores made me want to melt away. The pressure of having so many lives resting on my shoulders made bile rise in my throat. My hands clenched and released at my sides. Baron stepped forward amongst the crowd and grabbed my hand, knowing the panic was rising within me. It shot through our bond like lightning. My body was rigid, and my heartbeat thumped as hard as Emeris's wings.

"My people! Please, gather!" As Baron spoke, his voice was loud and calm. Murmurs along the worn paths through our village slowly grew more and more silent until the only noise was the branches of the trees swaying in the wind.

"Ember is approaching our shores." The gasps of fear and inaudible whispers started up again in a panic as Baron continued to speak. "We must remain calm, keep our heads clear." He paused, letting his words sink in. "They have initiated the war against all of Osparia, and we must prepare ourselves for what's coming. Gather our men and any women who want to join the fight. Step up." Multiple familiar faces stepped forward to the front. "We have something on our side that Ember won't be expecting." Everyone looked around a moment; confusion curled their brows while Baron glanced at me to tell them about Emeris.

I looked at the men and women I had known my whole life, not knowing how to explain to them that the creatures they had taught us to fear weren't threats. I felt the words caught somewhere between my throat and my mouth, but was unable to say them. Instead, I showed them. I looked up, making the whistle that called Emeris to me. For a few heartbeats, there was nothing but silence as everyone looked around with their eyes filled with wonder until they heard her. The deep rumble of a roar as the air from her wings moved through the treetops, and she landed right behind Baron and me.

The men and women drew their swords and axes. Fear lined their faces, but Baron held up his muscled arm, stopping them as they stared at the scene in front of them: me, petting Emeris's chest as she brought her neck down to hug me. Everyone looked in awe at how close I was to her massive frame as her yellow eyes gleamed in their direction, looking over all of them. Her deep breath kicked up the dirt at all of our feet. My gaze darted around the crowd of my people, roaming over their faces before looking back up to Emeris.

Her posture was unyielding with nerves. For a moment, the only noise was our heavy breathing until I caught a glint of metal in my side view, but it was already too late. One warrior, known as Ravi, rushed forward, axe drawn for Emeris. The dragon pulled back, lowered her snout to her neck while she puffed out her chest, preparing for a battle. My pulse thrummed; my mouth went dry. I jerked to the left, where Ravi was coming from, blocking his battle-axe from Emeris's side. I brought my foot up to his chest and knocked him to the ground.

"She is not your enemy!" I heaved, anger flooded my senses at how quick Ravi was to think I would do anything to harm my people by bringing Emeris here. He kicked out his boot, hitting my ankles, knocking me to my back. He got back to his feet while Emeris lunged forward for him until a small voice coming low from the ground stopped her.

"Daddy!" the child screamed, squeezing from the safety of her mother's arms. Her mother's eyes were wide with terror, and she tried to chase after her baby trying to get to Ravi. The only thing standing between this father and his daughter was Emeris. Ravi raised his blade before I could scream.

Baron ripped the axe from his hand, tossing it to the loose soil. He placed his two hands on Ravis's shoulders, restraining him.

"No!" the mother cried from the crowd that held her back as Ravi jerked and pushed forward, but Baron gripped him firmly. The young girl stood there trying her best to be brave—unafraid, as Emeris lowered her head down to hers. The girl stood still, rooted to the ground with fear. Her chest heaved so hard, her whole body quaked until Emeris nudged her, gently showing affection. Emeris's head was bigger than the child's body. The girl held up her arms, her tiny hands barely able to cover the tip of her snout. Emeris released a huff of ashes and smoke from her nostrils, making the young girl giggle. The smokey air tousled her long blonde hair back over her shoulders, and it was as if the entire world went silent. My heart froze and my breath stalled as I looked from Ravi to his wife, Elise, to the crowd of our people. Their posture stiffened, eyes wide. Some had splayed fingers over their chests and mouths open in amazement at what they were witnessing. I rose to my feet, walking to where the little girl stood with a small smile spread over her face as Emeris nudged and played with her. Every breath Emeris took whipped at her blonde hair. Ravi and Elise stepped forward.

"She is not our enemy," I whispered, my voice breathy. I held out my hand to Ravi and his wife. Both of them lifted their arms with me, slowly placing their hands on Emeris's forehead as their young daughter played with the end of her snout. I looked at them and then at the crowd. My eye contact was unwavering. My stance was open, my head held high—confidence laced every word.

"The dragons are not our enemies. They love this land just as much as we do and will protect it just as we are. We don't have the power of the elements like most fae, but we all have the heart of the dragons on our side." My voice bellowed out through the crowd and Emeris lifted her head, releasing a loud purr like a calling to the sky. The ground shook and the winds grew until the trees whipped and the dust swirled around us. Looking up, all I could see were wings and scaled skin of all shades of color.

Dragons. An entire thunder of them. I'd seen glimpses of other dragons while flying with Emeris, but never like this.

Never this many.

I'd traveled through our islands and I'd never found their resting place or seen so many at once.

One by one, they all landed, circling my people as if they listened to Emeris's call to them. I took them all in, and Baron stood next to me. He intertwined his fingers with mine as Ravi grabbed his daughter and wife and they stepped back into the crowd. Eyes of all shades looked at me, blues, greens, yellows, and I swore one even had violet eyes beaming at me. They all bowed their heads to the ground, facing Baron, Emeris, and me. I squeezed Baron's hand as we both looked up at Emeris. She gave us a strong, decisive nod before she thrust out her chest, standing tall amongst the bowed dragons.

It took me a moment to understand, but soon I realized.

She chose us. The dragons had chosen us. They wanted to fight for their home just as much as we did.

I held my chin high as I spoke. "Listen to your chieftess. We misjudged the dragons. These creatures have a heart of passion and fire, just like us. Let us help each other protect our lands and our home!"

I unsheathed my sword. Baron followed my lead, and we lifted them above both of our heads, waiting for our people's response. Our men, women, and warriors did the same with their axes, daggers, and pitchforks, gradually chanting something to themselves until they all grew louder and louder.

"Dragonheart, Dragonheart, Dragonheart!" The moment brought a lump of emotion to my throat. Pride beamed from my chest at seeing my people unified with the beasts they'd once hunted. Emeris lifted her head toward the skies, letting out a bellowed roar. She quaked the very ground I stood on before bringing her head back down, rubbing the side of her head against Baron and me.

"Ember will be here at daybreak, but we'll be waiting." The cheers of our people roared along with the dragons of Osparia, filling my heart with something I hadn't felt in a while—hope.

CHAPTER FOUR

"A ny women or elders not fighting gather the children and go with Shay to find refuge off the island." Baron's voice boomed through our village, reaching all ears. Every fae glanced up at Baron as fear struck their faces. Who could blame them?

There was a war landing on our beaches and we'd never left the shores of our islands before. At least not for long. I stepped forward, giving them warm smiles, trying to reassure them. Baron put his hand on the small of my back as he spoke. "Ember will be here at daybreak. We must prepare for tonight! Set the traps. Archers, take posts in the highlands. We must protect our home." Our people scattered, ready to do their duties before dawn.

Most of the dragons launched back into the skies as if they understood the commands. The few that stayed behind dropped themselves to the ground, making it easier for us to climb onto their backs. I glanced at Emeris, and she scaled down as well for me to get on, but I couldn't leave before the others. I walked over to the small group of fae that wouldn't be fighting, slowly helping them get atop the dragons' backs. The children were excited to be on the dragons. While it took the few elders some time to get up, they were still leery about the winged beasts.

Being fae, they were quite agile for their years in this world. I peered over, seeing Ravi saying goodbye to his wife and daughter as he helped them up.

"You can stay with them, you know," I said, and he just shook his head.

"I am with them in fighting for a home to return to."

I gave him a smile and nodded, feeling proud of how far he had come in such a short time.

"Hold on tight," I declared to everyone on the dragons before whistling my bird song, sending them all gently into the skies. I turned to Ravi.

"I'm going with them to be sure they get someplace secure. Go meet Baron. He'll tell you what to do next."

"Thank you."

"Don't thank me yet."

"Then promise me . . ."

"Ravi—" He cut me off.

"Ensure that if anything happens, you'll keep them safe." I knew he was referring to his wife and daughter. My heart couldn't turn down a man's last wish for his family, so I tried to give him hope to cling to.

"They will make it through this, and you will too. No goodbyes yet." He gave me an enduring look before following the warriors tending to their duties. I ran to Emeris, leaping on her backside as she darted up through the trees, pursuing the other dragons off the coast of the isle.

Staying toward the rear, I could see the children spreading their arms out into the open as the breeze whipped their hair. It brought a smile to my face, hearing the faraway sounds of their laughter. The sun was barely a sliver above the distant dark waters below. As the dragons flew forward, the islands spread out so small behind us that I grew confused.

"Emeris . . . where are you going?" She huffed a breath, and I looked forward, trying to see through the growing mist. Wondering where the land had gone, I glanced back again, not seeing the Espien Islands anymore. Mist and fog grew as thick as smoke. The weight of it pushed against my skin as if flying through a barrier of some sort. The tang of magic filled the air. My nose burned as it tingled through me, making the hairs on my neck raise. Everything in my gut told me to turn away, but Emeris flew onward. I tried to tug on her to get her to turn, but she wouldn't listen to me.

"Emeris! Turn back!" I yelled over the whistling wind, but all she did was purr loudly, trying to calm me. I looked around. The fog had grown so thick, I couldn't see the other dragons anymore nor hear the laughter of the children. My heart thrummed with the prickly feeling of fear growing, making my stomach churn. My head pounded as my ears popped under the pressure. The urge to run tightened through every muscle in my body. I held my breath a moment, fighting my body's desire to turn away, and then as fast as the pressure and dread had built against me, it fell aside, gone as the fog lifted and the dark sky grew clear. Looking down, my eyes found an island I'd never seen before, and now I realized why. Magic protected it. Powerful magic that I had never felt before. This wasn't like elemental bending. It was different—old.

It was an ancient type of illusion I didn't know existed anymore, similar to a fae glamour but more formidable. It left me feeling in awe of the amount of power it would take to glamour an entire island. All fae could glamour looks and feelings or anything about themselves, really, even someone or something in the same vicinity as them, if needed. But nothing as large as a piece of land.

Emeris landed along the shore with the other dragons. Mothers and children climbed down from the dragons they were riding. The magic still masked all their faces with fear from coming through whatever barrier protected this place. Emeris nudged me, making me walk forward as she tried to lead me through the trees. I turned to my people.

"Stay here until I come for you. The dragons will keep you safe." Everyone nodded in agreement as Emeris kept nudging me forward through the dense woods off the beach. There were no trails or signs of life. It seemed no one had been here for a time. Emeris led me through the large trees, and my curiosity got the best of me. That was when I noticed it: a vast, stone-looking building to my right. Vines growing so dense around it made it look like the world was dragging it underground. I veered to it, but Emeris stepped in front of me, stopping me from going any farther, and then I realized why . . . I saw him.

A dragon was lying on the top of it and staring down at me with his icy, fierce eyes. His coloring was something I'd never seen. His gilded scales shimmered against the moonlit forests, almost making him look as if he were a statue made of gold perched atop the building to scare away anyone who'd want to go inside. They'd get an awakening if they tried. He nodded to Emeris as if telling her to keep moving, and I was not going to disobey. I saw a small mountain in the distance and dark shadows of wings in the air. When I looked farther ahead of me, I could see the trees grow scarce as a cave-like hole opened on its side—nothing but darkness. Emeris opened her mouth, creating a faint glow of the fire from her throat, giving us a light source as we stepped into the cavern after walking for what seemed like forever with only hearing my heart pounding in my ears. I heard the rustling sounds of wings, the popping of fire on wood, and a warm orange glow came from up ahead. I ran to it, the suspense of not knowing where I was taking over. Rushing through the opening with Emeris on my heels, I saw all the dragons that had landed on the isle were here, some flying, playing, others eating fish or some other animal carcass for dinner. This was their home.

The dragon's den.

Baron and I always knew there had to be one somewhere, but we never thought they would protect it on its own island, lying in the middle of the sea.

Children's laughter came echoing from my left, and I turned to see the other two dragons that flew here with us gliding through a different tunnel in the mountain before they landed in front of me. The children leapt down with their mothers, asking if they could ride again, while other children were yawning, rubbing their sleepy eyes. Emeris blew a thin line of fire to her right, and a row of flames licked up the side of the wall, slowly wrapping around until the room was lit with the warm glow of fire. It made it easier to see in the depths of this hollow mountain. I ran my hand over the wall closest to me, realizing that it was stone, too, just like the structure that the other dragon was resting upon.

"What is this place?" I whispered to myself, not expecting a response, but a raspy warm voice called back.

"This is Magni Island, where the mighty roam."

I jerked my head toward Emeris, with my eyes going as wide as saucers. She looked at me, and I was astonished by what I had heard. "Ris, did you just speak to me?"

"Yes," she hissed.

"That's impossible . . . I'm losing my mind."

"No, darling, Magni Island holds a lot of special qualities, one being that you can hear me in your mind if I choose."

"Amazing." I walked to her, running my hand down her neck and chest.

"Why is this place protected? Who is the golden dragon?" Questions spewed from my mouth faster than my thoughts could process.

"That's Draken. He's the last of his kind, and his story is not mine to tell."

"Are they safe here?" I glanced over to the women, children, and elders who had made their way farther into the vast expanse, lounging around a small fire and collecting the belongings they could bring on their person to use to sleep for the night.

"Yes, but Draken will only allow your welcome for so long. Come now, we must get back. My voice only works here. But I can still understand when you speak to me."

"It would've been nice to talk to you when we first met. Maybe we wouldn't have tried to kill each other." I gave her a small smile, and she gave me a side-eye, but I could hear her faint laugh in my head.

"Come on," she spoke to me from mind to mind, and I listened, getting up on her back.

"Shay! Where are you going?" Ravi's wife, Elise, yelled from across the room, and I reassured her before Emeris spread her wings to take off.

"You're safe here. I'll be back!"

Emeris launched us into the sky, barreling through one of the multitude of tunnels out of the side of the mountain before we soared through the night back home.

CHAPTER FIVE

I walked back to our cottage with exhaustion sinking into my bones, but my mind raced with all the thoughts of everything that had happened in one day. How much life could change in a blink of an eye.

As immortal fae, time was infinite. But when your entire world was on the cusp of war, it made every moment that much more precious.

I walked through the door. The smell of cooked meat and bread caught me off guard, making my stomach grumble. But a sweeter, familiar, exotic floral scent mixed with the ocean breeze made me turn my head. I wasn't expecting Baron to be home with what was coming at dawn, but I felt his calloused hands as they covered my eyes from behind me and I leaned back into his hard chest.

"What's all this?" I asked as a smile spread across my cheeks.

"Dinner with your favorite person who's not a dragon," he crooned in my ear, his voice low and soft. He kept my eyes covered but placed a kiss on my neck, and a shiver licked down my spine. "I have a surprise for you."

"Wait, I have to tell you about—"

He turned me around to face him, placing his forefinger over my lips. "You can tell me later," he whispered.

The gravelly sound of his voice made heat rise to my cheeks as I leaned in to kiss him. His finger glided down my bottom lip, past my chin, to the center of my chest, running between my breasts.

"Not yet." But he leaned in and placed a gentle kiss on my lips, anyway. "I got something for you. Close your eyes." I did as he asked. As he walked to the other room, I could hear his steps along the floor. "Keep them closed," he demanded as he called over his shoulder, catching me peeking.

"Okay, okay, they're closed." I obeyed, squeezing my eyes shut, giggling to myself.

"Okay, open." I opened my eyes to a full bouquet of violet hyacinths. Bright purple blooms popped from all directions of the stalks he held in front of me. Their scent filled the room and made me remember the smell from when I walked in.

"How did you get these?!" I squealed.

"I took a small trip today to find them," he said.

"Small? Baron, these don't grow anywhere near here. You didn't have to do this! They're beautiful, thank you." Violet hyacinths grew on one of the secluded small islands of Espien, only blooming once a year. Their rare beauty had always been something I loved. I placed them in a small clay vase on the table where dinner was already sitting before turning back to Baron.

"I wanted to be sure you got to see them one last time before tomorrow." A heavy silence weighed between us for a moment at the thought of tomorrow before he stepped up to me. He wrapped an arm around my waist, holding it at the small of my back while he brought his other hand up to cup my cheek. He pulled me into a passionate kiss. His hand slid to the nape of my neck as he started trailing kisses down my jawline, to my neck. He pulled the straps of my blouse downward to glide his lips down my chest. A breathy hum of pleasure escaped from me; my body clenched with need from all his small touches.

I nibbled my lip as Baron licked and sucked on my peaked nipples before he slowly ripped the rest of my shirt off so he could move down to my torso. He paused, looking up at me through his light lashes, and grinned wolfishly.

Undoing my leathers, he pulled them to the ground. I stood completely bare to him. "I love the sounds you make from my touch." His voice skidded over my middle as he dropped lower, and my breath hitched at feeling his warm breath against my inner thighs. I bit down harder on my bottom lip.

"Don't hold back, love." His husky voice vibrated across my center. Teasing with his hot tongue, his mouth lingered and kissed over my folds. As his breath skittered over my opening, I arched into him, feeling the first touch of his tongue inside me. Licking me up and down made my legs give out from under me. Crazed sensations pulsed through me as Baron pushed me back against the door of our home, and my legs wrapped around his bare shoulders as he devoured me. My head fell back; panted breaths turned to loud moans. Liquid heat pooled in my center from craving him, all of him. Baron didn't relent. He wrapped his hands around my hips, gripped my ass, and pushed himself farther between my thighs, licking and suckling at my small bundle of nerves. Faster, harder, he sent an uproar of tingling fire through my limbs. I writhed farther into his mouth, the euphoria building unbearably high as I threaded my hands in his long hair.

"Baron!" I screamed his name as my release shuddered through my whole body, making my hips buck against him as I cried out. He ground against my core, sucking and lapping until my screams were nothing but small moans and heaving breaths. Baron kneeled, bringing me back down to the ground from the wall he had pinned me against. Bringing my legs down from his shoulders, I leaned against the wall, trying to regain my composure on shaky legs. He slowly kissed his way back up my body before he found my lips. Seeing his eyes filled with heat as his hard length pushed against my front, my body reacted, ready for him, ready for more. I opened my mouth, letting our tongues explore as I tasted my bliss still gleaming on his lips. Baron lifted me without breaking our passionate kisses and carried me to our bed.

"If tonight is our last, then we're not leaving this bed until dawn." He undid his trousers, yanking them down before he crawled up between my legs like a feral animal stalking its prey. Feeling his hardened length tip into my center made me squirm. His body weight pressed down onto me, fitting perfectly between my thighs. I rolled my hips into his, craving his touch, desperate with need. I wrapped my legs around his waist, positioning him at my entrance. He thrust into me deep and slow. His movements were steady, rolling long strokes. He made sweet love to me as he trailed kisses up my neck and back and across my jawline until his lips finally claimed mine. He slid out almost to his tip, painfully slowly, before he thrust deeply into me again. His tender pace filled my body with a carnal need for more. A throaty moan escaped me as our lips broke apart.

"Baron—please," I begged as he looked down at me with a teasing grin.

"How bad do you want it, love?" he questioned breathlessly as I grabbed his hips, pulling him deeper, harder into me, insistent that he move faster. A low moaned laugh escaped him as he obeyed my desires. His body rolled with mine, demanding, claiming, wanting.

His mouth swallowed my cries of pleasure. As I writhed harder against him, unable to control my movements, I grabbed and scratched at his muscled back. His thrusts quickened, inching us both to the edge. Our movements became frenzied. Baron wrapped his hands in my braids, clutching against my scalp, pounding deeper into me. The guttural noises we made for each other became raw and feral—unworldly. My body tightened against his, and I closed my eyes, letting my body begin to fall over the ledge into euphoric bliss again.

"Look at me," Baron groaned, his voice guttural. "I want to watch you come undone."

His body went rigid against mine, his veins bulging as he tightened his grip on my hair and slammed into me, our skin slapping. I cried out as my climax coursed through my limbs. Hot wetness pooled between my thighs as Baron's release spilled into me while he watched me.

The fiery buzz clawed through my nerves. Our breaths were heavy pants as he dropped his head into the crook of my shoulder. I tried to calm my racing heart. Baron slipped himself out of me. Leaning over to the side, he brought his hand up to my dewy face and brushed a thumb over my rosy cheeks.

"You're breathtaking."

Being mated, the love I had for this man was indescribable—all-consuming. I could only say three words, but no matter how many times I said them to him, they would never be enough.

"I love you, Baron," I whispered in a shaky breath. He leaned over, placing a soft kiss on my full lips.

"I love you too, Shay." His voice was raw and thick with emotion. Knowing what awaited us at dawn made it that much more meaningful. If I could pause and stay in this moment for the rest of eternity, I would. But we didn't have the luxury of time anymore.

In between a night filled with lust and love, sleep found me. When I woke, Baron was sitting up in bed. He had been running his fingers loosely through my small braids while I slept.

"Did you get any rest?" I asked, my voice still filled with sleep as I looked up at him.

"No." His eyes never met mine. He observed his fingers roaming through my hair instead of meeting my gaze.

"You should have gotten some rest."

"I couldn't sleep." His voice was low, and his shoulders sagged.

"Baron—" I sat up, stopping him, forcing him to look at me. "—you sound as if we've already lost."

"Ember is powerful, Shay. We've seen what they are capable of after what they did to Heavensreach. They destroyed an entire race just to kill one Sky Elf they felt was in their way."

"We can't just cave. We have to try and fight."

"We will." His voice graveled through his chest before it broke. "But if things go amiss . . ."

"Baron, don't—" He silenced me with his touch as one of his hands came up to cup my face.

"Shay." His eyes pierced mine, his features growing more serious. "I will watch this world fall before I lose you."

I turned my cheek into his hand, kissing his palm. "You won't lose me."

"You're right. I won't allow it." Heat reddened my cheeks as my lips curved up at his sincerity. Something caught my attention out of the corner of my eye. Specks of darkness fell from the sky through our window. I looked at Baron, brow already furrowed, realizing what was happening. We both quickly got up and gathered our clothes. As Baron prepared himself, so did I. I shimmied my thick hips into my tight leathers, laced my daggers to my thighs and across my chest, and strapped my sword to my side. I placed my bow and arrow on my back. We both looked at each other when we were done, our faces strained, ready for war.

As we stepped outside, other warriors were already getting into their positions, some still restless from a night of no sleep. Black soot slowly blanketed the ground like the first snow of winter. The warships that burned through coal were so close now, you could see them lined against the orange glow of the horizon. The charcoal stench rained down like a cloud of terror, foreshadowing the destruction before it fully arrived.

Ember was encroaching on our shores, and they were thirsty for blood.

CHAPTER SIX

The metal tang of ships as they ground against our shores hurt my ears until they came to a screeching hold. Baron left me with a kiss before he joined our warriors on the ground. I took aim from one of the taller trees. I'd always been best with a bow. Drawing it up, I focused on where the blackened ships sat, sinking into the sands. I waited for their spiked point at the tip of the ship to lower, revealing its insides where Ember fae soldiers would march down from onto the water's edge.

The creak of the metal pulled my attention to the ship in the middle of the five sitting on our island. As the metal tip lowered, I tightened my grip on my arrow, preparing myself for what was to come. As the door thudded on the beach, a single set of footsteps echoed against the ore. A woman came walking out, her hair as black as the soot falling from the ships she sailed from. Her skin was paler than I expected. Her black boots laced above her knee. I could barely tell the difference between her boots and pants as they matched perfectly. Her top was lower cut with a fitted jacket over top with accents of blood red along the sides of her torso and sleeves. She walked out, calm and alone. Confident in every move she made. Calculated. Unafraid and deadly.

As the doors opened on the other ships, Fire Fae soldiers came out in a single file line. They joined her, all of them stopping a few feet behind her, waiting for her orders to strike.

I watched as her murky amber eyes scanned the wood line. Her eyes looked as if they matched the color of all the blood she'd spilled against innocent soil. She huffed, almost as if she felt bored.

"I believe I'm looking for Baron," she spoke loud enough for any fae to hear. "Or is it Shay I should ask for? Where I'm from, women have, oh what's the word . . ." She hummed to herself as if this were some sort of game. "Sway, with authority." A few tense moments passed, and she tapped her forefinger against the hilt of her sword like she was growing impatient about nothing exciting happening yet. Baron stepped out from the tree line, his stance tense as the woman's posture shifted toward him. "Ah, you must be the great Baron, the Dragon Slayer of Espien. I've heard good things."

"Cut the shit. Who are you, and what do you want?"

"Oh, you're brave, and cute." Her lip curled to the side as Baron bared his teeth. He took a step in her direction. The soldiers all turned in complete unison as their arms caught ablaze with bright-red fire, and my heart fell from my chest. I hoped Baron would step down. He stopped in his tracks as the woman continued. "I see being on an insignificant piece of land, word must not travel here very well, so allow me to introduce myself . . . I'm Valla Corvus, Princess of Ember, Commander of armies, but you can call me Val." She walked nonchalantly. Every step she took closer to Baron made my heart skip and my stomach recoil. "Pleased to make your acquaintance." She did a small dip of her head before continuing. "I'm feeling kind today, so it is simple, really. You can either leave willingly and let Ember claim this land, or you can decline and burn." She looked him up and down, lifted a single brow as smugness leaked from her pores. "I'll even give you a few moments to decide."

Baron looked down at her, Valla's height right at the center of his chest, but this woman wielded power as if just one glance could set the universe on fire at her command. Baron's chest heaved. I watched him fight the urge to strike her down where she stood, but he knew the soldiers would attack relentlessly. He tore away from her gaze and turned back to the woods to find me. I threw my bow to my backside and slid down the tall tree. Baron was tense, his words fast, "Shay . . . what do you want us to do?"

"We have a dragon's heart, remember? I say we fight." He shook his head, knowing just how outnumbered we were. Just the rows of soldiers from five ships outnumbered us. We'd be fighting two to one with no elemental bending abilities. It sounded like a death wish. But at least we'd be fighting for our homelands instead of running. Osparia was going to war, and we would have all faced this fight eventually. Baron's eyes met mine. "Our people know the stakes and want to fight because this is their home. We have to try." Baron huffed a breath, and I glanced back at the rows of Ember soldiers.

Val had unsheathed her sword, crossed her legs, and lightly leaned against it as she glanced at her nails, uninterested. Her confidence just made anger scorch through my veins. How she felt she could just show up and take whatever land she walked on. Her firm conviction of victory, I guessed, taking Heavensreach, made her cocky, or maybe she had always been this cunning. Baron signaled the archers to aim for their marks, and I saw a small curve of Val's lips in the distance, almost like she craved the violence of war, the thirst for blood, the destruction from the very flames she wielded.

The moment Baron moved, the sounds of arrows whistled through the air. Fire erupted into a tall wall in front of the soldiers from a flip of their wrists. Some arrows made it through before the flames licked up from the sands, the fatal hits of the arrows piercing the few Fire Fae soldiers straight through their hearts, giving them no time to recover and heal before their chests stopped heaving and death found them. Their blood slowly seeped into the sand, staining it, marking this place for war.

Val stepped through the flames right before the wall fell behind her with her sword drawn and her eyes wild, thirsty for devastation, like a leech needing blood to live. She rushed forward with her soldiers as our warriors broke through the tree line, swords drawn, daggers flying. The sounds of metal and tearing flesh filled the air shortly before the crackling, snapping sounds of the roaring blaze of flames danced across the land.

Ember fae had no restraint as they whirled fire from their fingertips. Burning flesh and ash assaulted my nose in the wind as I ran into battle. I pulled my bow back with three arrows, shooting three enemy soldiers straight through their chests with deadly precision before throwing my bow and grabbing for my daggers across my chest. Sweat beaded my brow, and my clothes stuck to my curves as sweat soaked through them.

One by one, I watched people I had grown up with over the years fall before the blades and flames. Each of them took Ember soldiers with them to death, but they still outnumbered us, no matter the loss they took. I threw my daggers across the battlefield one by one. They hit their marks, sinking into a chest or a neck. I was sure to not give the enemy enough time to restore themselves. I could hear Baron calling for me through the depths of the roaring flames, but I had set my sights on one person.

Val.

I watched her walk through the flames as if she were forged from hell itself. Her eyes glowed against the bright oranges and reds flowing across the island. "You should have left when you had the chance," she said calmly, "but I'm glad you didn't. I like the fun." She teased about death as if it would never claim her.

I moved at fae speed, not giving her the chance to continue her spew. But with a slight curve of her body, she dodged both daggers, leaving me with only my sword left. Baron's calls came from a distance. I could feel him tugging on our bond, but my focus never left Val's face. I blocked my mind, my bond, to Baron's call to remain focused.

"I'll do you a favor. I'll make it even, no bending." Her smile devious, she drew up her sword, getting into a fighter's stance. Her movements were fast, lethal. Every move was obsessively precise. I could tell Val had spent her life perfecting her combat and bending skills. It was why she was a princess leading her empire's army.

I wasted no time thrusting my sword forward as the metal clanked and hissed against each other. With every strike, Val blocked and weaved past everything I threw at her until she pushed her sword forward, coming straight for me. I jumped to the side, swinging my sword down with all of my body weight onto hers, knocking it from her hands. I swung my sword up so fast she didn't have the chance to miss it as it grazed her face. Blood trailed down her cheek. She stumbled back. I rushed her, but fury filled her eyes as she lifted them back to mine.

"You think you stand a chance against Ember?" She wiped at her bloodied face. "These were just the leading ships of our fleet, you fool!" A manic laugh escaped her as her hands glowed a bright blue. Lightning popped and cracked between her fingertips, preparing to shoot forward straight into me. Her bending was so concentrated, she'd learned to wield beyond her fire—lightning.

My eyes went wide. Baron cried out to me, but he was too far away battling Ember soldiers in the distance, bobbing and weaving their flames. I could sense my end coming until a black-winged figure caught my eye, soaring down through the flames. She whipped the Princess of Ember back away from me with her long tail. I jumped, climbing onto her back, heaving breaths as adrenaline pulsed through my veins.

I coughed as the smokey air became crisp in the open sky. Rubbing my hand down Emeris's neck, I thanked her for saving me. "I owe you for that one," I rasped. Her low growling purr was her only response as we circled back.

Val's claim came into view. Ember lined the horizon with dozens more of black warships.

"These were just the leading ships of our fleet, you fool!" Her voice echoed in my mind. *We have to get out of here.* But my thought wasn't faster than Val's lighting as she launched it at me. The slightest hint of her defeat in our battle earlier infuriated her. Emeris banked hard to the right. The lightning gashed through her side, causing her to roar, bellowing out in pain. She free fell a moment before regaining herself, her flight wobbly as her wound gushed. Her body trembled as if the lightning were still sizzling

through her limbs. More dragons fell to their end as Val unleashed her rage.

I veered Emeris toward the far end of the island, landing where Ember had yet to reach. I leaped down hastily, moving to check her injuries. Her low bellow of pain made me wince as I assessed the damage.

"Will you be alright?" The fear of losing her laced in my tone. She just looked at me and gave me a nod. "Can you fly? Will the others help us escape?" Her only response was a loud roaring purr as she called out to the other dragons. Within a few moments, I watched as more of them appeared as if they were emerging from the clouds from beyond the waters. From Magni.

"Wait for my signal. I've got to get us out of here. It's over." I placed my forehead against hers, bidding her farewell for now as I rushed back into the tree line. The heat of the flames found me quickly. They snapped and whooshed as trees fell, gasping as the roar of the flames consumed them, sucking away their life. My eyes burned not only from the smoke, but the turmoil building behind them. The realization that I had failed my people. Not only did I lose lives, but we all lost our home.

My breath quickened as I rushed through the black smoke. The screams and cries of death resonated around me. Bile rose in my throat at the smell of burning flesh and iron soaked into the surrounding fumes, but I couldn't tell if it was from the blood or the heated metal of the swords.

I heard my name rasped from a body lying on the ground in the distance. The sound made me stop in my tracks. My heart stuttered over itself. No, no, no . . . My mind already understood as my heart strained to comprehend. To believe.

Ravi lay before me. A sword was pierced through his gut and burns covered over half of his body. Tears slipped from my eyes. I could no longer hold them back as I fell to my knees next to him. "You're going to be okay. You're going to be okay." Disbelief was always the first stage of grief before understanding.

All he did was shake his head, gasping for the very breath his lungs were trying to cling to. He unsheathed a dagger from his thigh with a trembling, charred hand. He grabbed me and placed the hilt into my palm, lacing my fingers with his around it. I knew what he was asking me to do. How could I kill one of my own even if I was putting him out of his misery? "I can't—I . . ." My words stumbled. I couldn't breathe through the smoke and fumes. Panic consumed me, but Ravi grabbed my arm.

"Please, it's over for me, Shay." His voice was low and graveled as he heaved for life in between his words. Blood trailed from his mouth. My heart splintered in my chest at his request, and my lungs burned from the broken pieces and the smoke that filled them.

"Promise me . . ." His voice wheezed. "Promise me . . . ," he repeated, tightening my hold on the dagger.

"I promise," I screamed, my throat raw, as I plunged the dagger into my fellow man's chest. His fingers went loose against my hand as his body relaxed. His eyes glazed over, empty of life.

My mind grew groggy—distant. The smoke consumed me as I tried to stand. I thought I walked, but speckles of black lined my vision, and then I felt the ash-covered ground under my hands. My body moved, crawled, as my mind went to a faraway place.

A name echoed through the flames from a familiar voice, my name, but I couldn't place where it was coming from. My vision faded as a heavy hand hauled me back up to my feet in my dazed state.

"Shay! We have to go! More are coming." Baron coughed over the roar of the heat. The flames pulled the life from everything near them. My body begged for water, for air, feeling almost numb to the heat now. I stumbled, falling forward into the ashes again. I could hear Baron curse under his breath, hauling me into his arms.

"Stay with me, Shay," was all I heard before my mind fell into nothingness.

CHAPTER SEVEN

I jolted awake, pushing my body up. I felt the wind rush over my face. Baron urged me back down, placing a wet rag over my forehead.

"Oh, thank gods." His voice shook, and I could feel the fear radiating down the bond that tethered us. He thought he was going to lose me. Emeris purred low and soothingly as we soared above the islands. Every breath burned as my body tried to recover from the smoke.

I leaned up slowly. This time I glanced alongside us, seeing more dragons carrying our soldiers, our people, but so many faces were missing. I closed my eyes, my brow furrowed as the image of Ravi sat in the forefront of my mind. What was I going to tell his wife and daughter? I was sure his wife felt the difference in the air, the break in their tether, as soon as he took his last breath.

A sob croaked out of me as tears slipped down my face. Baron sat behind me. He wrapped his arms tightly around my chest, holding me against him as if he could mend all my broken pieces back together again. My body shook as I gasped and heaved through my tears. If he was crying too, I didn't know, but his breathing was uneven against my neck as he let me weep. I turned to face him. Our eyes matched with the same sorrow. I'd failed Baron, my people, the dragons. We'd lost our home.

"I'm sorry," I rasped. "I failed us." He cupped my ash- and tear-smeared face.

"No, we never fail, love. We either win or we learn." His lip trembled as he placed a soft kiss on my forehead before leaning his against mine.

I glanced down at the Espien Islands, now engulfed in flames. A figure stood on the shores, her dark hair lightly shifting in the warm breeze. Val stood there watching as we flew through the skies. Her chest heaved from exhaustion from the amount of power she had used. But I could've sworn she carried a wicked, victorious smile on her face, knowing she had won this battle.

My heart became determined, seared with the loss of my people and home. The silence of death hung in the wind as I made a promise to myself. We'd lost this battle, but we would be there for the end of this war. And we would find peace again.

To be continued...

To find out where Shay and Baron end up, purchase book one of
The Osparia Series:

Fate of Water and Wind

THANK YOU

If you enjoyed The Osparia Series Novellas please consider
leaving a review on:
Goodreads, Amazon, or your personal social media.
and follow along with Lashell's author journey.
Her next release is book one of the series:
Fate Of Water And Wind

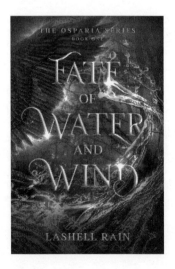

ACKNOWLEDGMENTS

Thank you to my beautiful children for being patient with me (or at least trying to be) as I wrote this story and continue to write new adventures.

To my mom; thank you for teaching and instilling in me that if you want something in life, you can't just wish it to be, you have to work hard to get it. I wouldn't be where I am today without that advice growing up.

To my brother; if you ever read this (that's doubtful) but if you do... no you didn't. Also, what's up?! Call me sometime, and we can hang out and go to Shell Shack together!

To the amazing community of friends I've made on TikTok; Thank you, from the bottom of my heart, for your support and for welcoming me into the bookish community. Without you, I wouldn't have ever published. You all inspired me to reach for the stars and write the dang thing!

To Norma Gambini from Normas Nook Proofreading; Thank you for all of your support and amazing eagle eyes!

To Lylah Taylor; Thanks for always listening to me rant about my books and helping me work through all the bumps in the road. To Miblart; Thank you for the beautiful cover!

ABOUT THE AUTHOR

Lashell Rain is a foodie fueled by a shameless amount of caffeine and a passion for storytelling. The Texas native lives at home with her two beautiful kids. Between being a mom by day, and a writer by night, she brought her dreams of becoming an author into a reality—by flying by the seat of her pants.

Made in the USA
Monee, IL
10 September 2022

13630155R00095